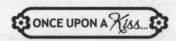

ONCE UPON A *Kiss*...

When ordinary girls get their fairy-tale endings!

Who says fairy stories can't come true?
Once Upon a Kiss... is our brand-new miniseries
featuring up-to-the-minute retellings of classic,
well-loved stories. Immerse yourself in a little bit
of fantasy for the modern-day girl, and be whisked
away, along with our down-to-earth heroines, to the
romances of your wildest daydreams!

This month's story is Shirley Jump's gorgeously
romantic *The Princess Test,* a retelling of
The Princess and the Pea, Princess Carrie Santaro has
always felt like an outsider in the palace.
Yet when she escapes and meets gorgeous single dad
Daniel, she realizes being a true princess takes more
than wearing a tiara....

Look out for the next timeless story in the series
by Fiona Harper,
coming soon!

Dear Reader,

I'm so thrilled to be back with the Santaro family, this time with feisty youngest sister, Carrie, who was great fun to write. I've always been a sucker for fairy tales (and will watch any movie based on a fairy tale), so putting my own spin on the classic *The Princess and the Pea* was both a challenge and a joy. Writing about princesses brings me right back to my childhood, when I used to pretend my dolls were marrying Prince Charmings of their own. My parents once bought me a Cinderella carriage with toy horses, and that became the primary mode of transportation for my white-dress-wearing dolls.

I do love to hear from readers, so please friend me on Facebook, visit my website, www.shirleyjump. com, drop me a line at P.O. Box 5126, Fort Wayne, IN, or stop by my blog at www.shirleyjump. blogspot.com to read about what I'm cooking tonight. Your emails and letters are truly the highlight of my day. It is such a thrill to share these characters with readers who love them as much as I do.

So welcome back to you, my dear readers, and to another member of the Santaro family! Happy reading!

Shirley

SHIRLEY JUMP
The Princess Test

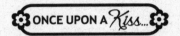
ONCE UPON A *Kiss...*

™
Harlequin®

TORONTO NEW YORK LONDON
AMSTERDAM PARIS SYDNEY HAMBURG
STOCKHOLM ATHENS TOKYO MILAN MADRID
PRAGUE WARSAW BUDAPEST AUCKLAND

Recycling programs
for this product may
not exist in your area.

ISBN-13: 978-0-373-17753-0

THE PRINCESS TEST

First North American Publication 2011

Copyright © 2011 by Shirley Kawa-Jump, LLC

New York Times bestselling author **Shirley Jump** didn't have the willpower to diet, nor the talent to master under-eye concealer, so she bowed out of a career in television and opted instead for a career where she could be paid to eat at her desk—writing. At first, seeking revenge on her children for their grocery-store tantrums, she sold embarrassing essays about them to anthologies. However, it wasn't enough to feed her growing addiction to writing funny. So she turned to the world of romance novels, where messes are (usually) cleaned up before The End. In the worlds Shirley gets to create and control, the children listen to their parents, the husbands always remember holidays and the housework is magically done by elves. Though she's thrilled to see her books in stores around the world, Shirley mostly writes because it gives her an excuse to avoid cleaning the toilets and helps feed her shoe habit. To learn more, visit her website at www.shirleyjump.com.

To my daughter, who may not be a frilly girl, but who is always the number-one princess in our house and in my heart.

CHAPTER ONE

DAWN broke its soft kiss over the lake, washing the blue-green water with a dusting of orange and gold. A slight breeze skipped gentle ripples across the water and whispered the scent of pine through the open window. Carrie Santaro curled up on the cushioned window seat, watching the day begin. In the three days since she'd arrived at her rented lakeside cottage in Winter Haven, Indiana, Carrie had spent every spare moment in this window seat, soaking up the tranquility and the quiet peace found in being utterly alone. Her sister Mariabella who lived half the year in a seaside town in Massachusetts had told her that life in the States was different from life in the castle.

She'd been right. Here, in this tiny Midwestern town with all its hokey charm, Carrie felt free. To be herself, to drop the mantle of her princess life and to be just… Carrie. To be the person she'd been fighting all her life to be. She hadn't packed a single ball gown, not one pair of high heels. While she was here, she'd be all jeans and T-shirts and sundresses all the time. Just the thought made her smile.

And while she was here, she decided, she'd find out who she really was. Maybe with enough distance between herself and the castle, she could finally get the answers she'd waited a lifetime to hear. After all, hadn't her mother once said that was what had happened to her when she'd visited this town? Perhaps Carrie could get lucky, too.

Her cell phone rang. She sighed before flipping it open and answering the call she'd been dreading. "Hello, Papa."

"Carlita!" Her father's booming voice, calling her by the name her parents used when they wanted to remind her of her royal roots—and royal expectations. To remind her she should be a dutiful daughter, an obedient princess.

Uh, yeah, not.

She'd always been a rebel, and never been much for the suffocating mantle of royal life. She was more at home with dirt under her nails than wearing a starched dress to a state dinner. She'd taken the etiquette lessons, suffered through boarding school and sat quietly through countless events, trying her best to be what everyone expected of a princess.

Most of the time. And now, she was doing the exact opposite, which had displeased her parents to no end. Carrie was tired of caring. She was ready to live her life and be free of all that once and for all.

"When are you coming home?" her father asked in their native, lyrical Uccelli language.

"I just got here," she answered, reverting to her native tongue, too. It felt a little odd after days of speaking only English. "I haven't even started working yet."

He pshawed away that notion. "You have work here. Come home."

"Papa, we talked about this. I'll be home in a few

months. The wine shop needs an advocate for Uccelli. If we can get the American sales off the ground—"

"We need you here," he said. "Your sisters, everyone, needs you here."

Ever since her middle sister, Allegra, had become queen, her parents had been urging Carrie to be a bigger part of the royal family, to take a more active role in the Santaro family causes and the country's needs. Something Carrie had resisted almost from birth. She wanted nothing to do with any of that. Just the thought of being surrounded by all that pomp and circumstance made her feel like she was being suffocated. "They're fine without me. I'm barely a part of the family activities. The media hardly noticed I left."

There'd been one small piece in the Uccelli papers, a quick mention that Princess Carlita had gone on vacation and nothing more, Mariabella had said. If Allegra had been the one to leave the country, there'd have been newspaper and television coverage for days. Not for the first time, Carrie thanked her lucky stars that she would probably never be queen.

"That's because we have worked to keep your 'antics' out of the media, and keep this vacation of yours a secret."

"It's not a vacation, Papa. It's a job."

He sighed. "I know you love this work, and think this is what you want to do—"

"*Think?* I know."

"But it is far past time you acknowledged your heritage," her father said. "And stopped playing in the vineyards. And at life. All these years, I have indulged you and let you have your freedom. You, of all the daughters, have had the least to do with the royal family and its duties. But now, you are twenty-four, my dear. Time to start settling down and become a true Santaro."

Settle down? She bristled at the thought of handing her life over to yet another person who would want to tell her where to sit, how to act, what she should do. In the past year, her father had reminded her a hundred times that playtime was over and now she needed to step more fully into her role as princess. "That is the last thing I want to do right now."

"I love you, my daughter, I really do, but you have one fault."

They'd had this discussion a thousand times and Carrie didn't want to have it again now. "Papa—"

"You flit from thing to thing like a butterfly. First it was wanting to be a landscaper. Then it was being a champion in dressage. Then it was rock climber, I think. Now, a shop owner." He paused, and she could hear the disappointment in his voice. "When are you going to settle down? It is time to be serious."

"I am, Papa."

He sighed. "I know you are trying, but it would be nice if you found a career you could stick with. A place to really shine."

"I already have—working in the vineyard." But as she said the words, she knew he had a point. She had darted from job to job, pursued a dozen careers in as many years. She'd never settled down with anything until now. Not a job, not a man, not a thing. "You don't understand. It's hard to find your place in the sun," she said quietly, "when there are so many stars overhead."

"Oh, *cara,* I understand that," her father said, his voice softer. "I grew up in my father's court, the second of five. If my eldest brother hadn't died, I would have lived a very different life than the one I had. It was a good life, though, and I am not complaining."

Carrie sent up a silent prayer that she was so far removed from the throne that she would probably never have to worry about wearing the crown. "I love working in the vineyards and with the wine, Papa. I want to run the vineyards someday."

"It is not a proper job for a princess," he said. "Go back to college. Become a doctor. A humanitarian. Something that befits royalty."

In other words, not something where she got her hands dirty. When the vineyard's marketing manager announced last month that this year's harvest would be his last because he was retiring, Carrie had seen it as her chance to take a more active role in the company she loved so much. Her father had disagreed. She'd hoped he would come around, but clearly, he wasn't about to. She wanted to prove to him with this trip that she could do both—have a career she loved and represent the royal family in a dignified way. "Papa, I will be home in a few months," she said again, more firmly this time.

"This is yet another lark for you, Carlita, my dear." Franco Santaro sighed. "I worry about you."

"You don't need to, Papa."

"I do, *cara*. You dropped out of college after your first year. Then dropped out of the second one. And barely finished at the third. And now you go to this town—" He cut off the sentence, leaving whatever else he intended to say unsaid. "I worry. That's all."

Carrie winced at the reminders. "I just wasn't a good fit for college. I love being outside, being hands-on." She sighed, then gripped the phone tighter. "Tell

Mama I love her. I have to go or I'll be late for work. I love you, Papa."

"I love you, too. I will talk to you soon."

Carrie hung up the phone. She showered and dressed, then drove the two miles from her rental house to the downtown area of Winter Haven. It wasn't until she parked that she realized she was a full half hour early for her first day of work.

She got out of the rental car and stood under the sign of By the Glass, the specialty wine shop where she'd be spending the end of summer and early fall. This was what it had all come down to—her years working in the vineyard, working her way up from a vineyard tech job to a viticulturist assistant, and after she'd gotten her degree, assistant to the manager.

She'd loved learning about the science of field blending to create new flavors. Loved seeing the finished product taken from a harvest and bottled for consumption. She'd tried several degree programs before settling on one in sales and marketing, with a heavy concentration in viticulture—even though her father had argued against those courses.

Once she got more hands-on at the vineyard, she wanted to parlay what she had learned into growth for the company. It had taken nearly a year to convince her father that Uccelli's amazing wines should be sold in the U.S. and that she should be the one to head the venture. When Jake, Mariabella's new husband, had offered backing to open a wine shop in the small tourist town in the Midwest, the former king of Uccelli had finally agreed.

At first, Carrie was content to let the shop run itself while she watched from Uccelli and spent her days helping the vineyard manager run the operation. But as the first few weeks passed and the sale of Uccelli wines in America remained stagnant, she knew she wanted to take a more active role. Do what made her happiest—get involved and get her hands dirty. And finally implement some of what she had learned in college.

She'd spent two weeks at a wine shop in Uccelli, learning the techniques of selling. Still, her father had had his doubts, sure she'd turn around in a day, a week, a month, and embark on something else.

How could she blame him? When she'd come home from her third and final college, her father had been sure she'd never settle into any one career, despite her framed degree. But Carrie had retreated to the vineyards, and as soon as she did, felt at home. She'd known this was where she'd been meant to be all along. Any doubts she might have had disappeared.

Now Carrie was going to prove not just her own worth as a vineyard director, but the worth of the Uccelli wines to foreign markets. And maybe, just maybe, she'd return to Uccelli, and her father would finally see she was committed to this work, and the best next choice to run the vineyard's overseas operations. If not, well, she'd scrimp and save until she had a vineyard of her own.

But the little nagging doubts still crowded on her shoulders. *What if you quit this, too?* that voice whispered. *What if you fail? Where will you be then?*

She would not fail. Simple.

Carrie unlocked the front door, let herself in, then did the few morning tasks required to open the store. By the time Faith, the regular clerk, came in, the shop was already humming with music and warm incandescent light. "Wow," Faith said as she dropped off her purse behind the counter. "You're in early."

"I was excited about my first day." Carrie slipped onto the other side of the heavy basket display of featured wines and helped Faith carry it out to the sidewalk. The salesclerk—whom Carrie had met when she'd arrived in Winter Haven on Friday—was a tall, thin blonde with a warm smile and wide green eyes. She'd welcomed Carrie, and quizzed her for a solid hour about the Uccelli wines that first day, clearly excited to meet someone who had direct experience with the vineyards.

"It's nice to work with someone who likes their job," Faith said as they walked back into the shop. "The last girl we had here was late so often I gave her an alarm clock for her birthday."

"Did it work?"

"Nope. She dropped it when she ran to her car that night because she was late for a date." Faith shook her head. "I already think you're going to be a better clerk than she ever was. Plus you know these wines better than anyone."

Carrie brushed away a long lock of dark hair, and tucked it behind her ear. A flush heated her cheeks. "Thank you."

"Hey, I'm having a party a week from this Friday," Faith said as she arranged a display of corks on a small round table by the register. "Just burgers and chips at my lake cottage before the weather gets too cold to do anything. You should come. You'll get to know a lot of the locals." Faith grinned. "Maybe even meet someone sexy for a little end of summer fling."

"A fling? Me?" Carrie laughed. "I'm not the fling type."

"Think about it. You have the perfect situation. You're only here for a few weeks before you go back to the other side of the world. What better time to have a fling?"

"Princesses don't have flings, Faith. My father would have a heart attack." She could just imagine Papa's face if she added a public scandal to her list of mistakes. It would be ten times worse than the time she skidded in a half hour late wearing grape-stained jeans to a media-filled dinner with the Prime Minister of Britain.

Faith leaned in closer to Carrie. "Every woman deserves a fling, Carrie. Otherwise, you'll end up married and surrounded by kids and wondering what the hell you missed out on."

Carrie thought of the prescribed life ahead of her. The people expected it, after all. Her oldest sister was married and already talking about kids, while her middle sister, the queen, had gotten engaged last month. Carrie was expected to go back to Uccelli, find an "acceptable" career, and an "acceptable" spouse, as her older sisters had done, and then fill her calendar with state dinners and ribbon cuttings and uplifting speeches.

Ugh. Just the thought of what lay ahead made Carrie want to run screaming from the room. How had her mother ever stood it? Was that why she'd reminisced about her time in Winter Haven? Because it had been a brief pocket of freedom to be herself?

"I'll be there," Carrie said, deciding that while she was here, she was going to experience everything she could. She might not have a fling, but she intended to have a damned good time. It might be her last opportunity for a while, and she intended to take advantage of the break from expectations.

Mama had told her dozens of times about this little Indiana town, a place she'd visited once when she'd been younger, before Carrie had come along. Mama had lived here for a summer under an assumed name, as a person, not as a queen. In those days, the media hadn't been as ravenous to uncover every detail, nor did they have the resources of the internet, so Bianca had been allowed a rare window of obscurity. Mama had raved about this town to Carrie so often that when Carrie was brainstorming with Jake about a test location in the U.S., Winter Haven had been the first one to come to mind. In the few days that she had been here, she had seen firsthand why her mother loved the little town so much. It was charming, quiet and filled with warm, welcoming residents.

And, to be perfectly honest, she'd wanted to know what the appeal had been for her mother. Whenever Mama talked about Winter Haven, her features softened, and she got this dreamy look. Carrie had to wonder what had made this place so unforgettable.

The morning passed quickly, with several customers coming into the little shop. Every bottle of Uccelli wine that left By the Glass gave Carrie a little thrill. It was like handing over a part of her heritage, herself, and she was delighted to share the beautiful bounty of her country with others. She belonged in this field, she just knew it.

By eleven, business had slowed. "You certainly have the magic touch," Faith said. "I don't think we've ever sold that much wine in the first two hours of being open."

"People must be in a wine buying mood."

"Or they're so dazzled by meeting a real-life princess that they buy every bottle they can."

"Oh, I don't know about that." Carrie had mentioned her royal heritage when people asked her about her accent, which wasn't all that pronounced, given the years she'd spent in British boarding schools—one of many attempts by her parents to curb their wild child. And even then, she'd released the information reluctantly, and only when pressed.

"I'm telling you, we should capitalize on the princess angle. Put up a sign and everything."

"Put up a sign?"

"Something small. No billboards or anything. This is a tourist town, and a little brush with a royal, that's the kind of thing tourists love."

She hesitated. "I don't know."

"Might as well flaunt it if you got it, sister." Faith grinned.

Advertise her royal heritage? Use it as a marketing tool? The idea grated. Her princess status had always been a chokehold on her freedom. "I just think it'd be better not to advertise that whole thing."

"It could sell a whole lot of wine," Faith said. "And isn't that your goal? To make this store a success?"

Confronted with that truth, Carrie really didn't have grounds to refuse. And wouldn't it be ironic if the thing she hated most about her life became the thing that helped her get what she wanted? Plus, if she handled it right, she could show her parents that Carlita Santaro was the perfect representative for the kingdom's wines.

Carrie glanced down at her faded jeans and the store logo T-shirt she was wearing. "I know one thing for sure."

"What's that?" Faith asked.

"I won't be the princess they're expecting."

Faith smiled. "And that's part of your charm."

Carrie reached over and plucked the chalkboard advertising today's specials out of the window. "So… where's the chalk?"

The sign worked wonders. As word spread about Carrie's presence in the shop, business began to triple, then quadruple. Carrie's naturally outgoing personality was a perfect fit for the curious tourists. Faith was over-the-moon ecstatic about the uptick in business, and started talking about bringing in some temps to help with the additional influx of customers. Every day, Carrie went home to her rented cottage by the lake, feeling satisfied and proud of the job she was doing.

Maybe now, after seeing how she had helped spur sales of Uccelli's prizewinning wines in America, her father would see that she was made for this business. That her heart was there, not in the palace or in some stuffy office.

"Hey, do you mind if I run out for lunch today?" Faith asked when business had ebbed a bit mid-Thursday morning. "I know we've been crazy busy, and I hate even asking, but my mom and sister are in town today and they want my input on planning my youngest sister's baby shower."

"Go right ahead," Carrie said. "I've got this under control." She cast a glance at the cash register that had been the bane of her existence ever since she'd started working here. She'd been able to do everything in the shop, except get the recalcitrant machine to do what she wanted. It seemed no matter which button she pushed, it was the wrong choice. "More or less."

Faith laughed. "Well, if it gets too crazy, just write down the sales and we'll run them through later. And remember, this button here—" she pushed a big green one "—will open the cash drawer."

Carrie nodded. "Okay. Got it."

After Faith left, Carrie got to work dusting the shelves and giving the display bottles an extra bit of polish while a few customers milled about the shop. On the center shelf, she picked up the signature wine from Uccelli—a graceful pinot grigio with notes of citrus and almond. Carrie knew it had a crisp, dry taste, one that seemed to dance on your tongue. Of all the wines manufactured on the castle grounds, this one was her favorite.

A sense of ownership and pride filled Carrie. She had tended these vines. She had picked these grapes. She had worked the machinery that took the grapes from fruit to liquid. For years, she'd been the rebel— the girl skidding in late to dinner, the one who'd ducked ribbon cuttings, the one who'd done whatever she could to avoid her identity and its expectations.

Funny how all that bucking tradition could result in something so sweet, so beautiful.

The label was decorated with an artist's rendering of the castle, its elaborate stone facade a dramatic contrast to the rustic landscape and the rocky shoreline. She traced the outline of the castle, ran her finger along the images of the four turrets, the bright purple-and-gold pennants.

The bell over the door tinkled. Carrie put the bottle back, then turned toward the door. A tall man stood just inside the entrance, his athletic frame nearly filling the doorway. The slight wave in his short dark hair accented the strong angles of his jaw. Sunglasses hid the rest of his features, yet gave him an edge of mystery. He had on jeans and a lightly rumpled button-down shirt, which made him look sexy and messy all at once.

Oh, my. Something in Carrie's chest tightened and she had to force herself to focus on her job, not on him. "Welcome to By the Glass," she said. "What can I help you find?"

He pointed toward the chalked sign in the window. "I'm looking for the princess."

Carrie smiled. She put out her arms and figured if this guy was disappointed to find out she wasn't a diamond-clad diva, that wasn't her problem. "That would be me."

He arched a brow. "You?"

"Yes." She put out a hand. She'd gotten used to introducing herself as a princess in the past few days, but this time, she hesitated for a second before speaking the words. Because she wondered what this handsome man's reaction would be? "I'm Carlita Santaro, third daughter of the king and queen of Uccelli. Which is where the grapes are harvested and the wines are bottled."

He removed the sunglasses, revealing eyes so blue, they reminded her of the ocean edging her home country. When he shook her hand with a strong, firm grip, Carrie thought about what Faith had said about having a fling. This guy was everything a woman looking for a little adventure could want. Tall, dark, handsome and with a deep voice that seemed to tingle inside her. And best of all, no wedding ring on his left hand.

"I'm sorry, but I was expecting someone more... formal."

She glanced down at the dark wash jeans and T-shirt

she was wearing, her bright pink shirt sporting a logo for the store, and laughed. "Princesses don't go around in long dresses and tiaras every day, you know."

"True." He released her hand, then fished in his breast pocket for a business card and handed it to her. "Daniel Reynolds. I work as a producer/reporter for *Inside Scoop.* I'd like to do a story on you and the shop."

"A…" She stared at the card, then at the man. "A story? For the news?"

"Well, the show I produce isn't news. Exactly." He let out a little cough. "We like to call it 'infotainment.'"

She shook her head. And here she'd actually been thinking of asking this man out. Clearly, her jerk radar was down, because this was just another vulture. "Paparazzi. Why am I not surprised?" She turned away from him, ignoring the business card. "Thanks, but no thanks." She crossed to a short, older woman who had entered the shop while they were talking, and started telling her about the shop's special on whites.

"I'm not a member of the paparazzi," he said, coming up behind her.

"This Riesling is one of our top sellers," Carrie said to the woman, ignoring him. He could spin it however he wanted, but she'd seen his type before. All they wanted was the scoop, another headline to blast across the airwaves. "If you like a sweeter wine, it's a great choice."

The woman tapped her lip, thinking. "I don't know. My tastes run in the middle, between dry and sweet."

"Then let me suggest—"

"This is the kind of story that could really put your shop on the map."

"—this pinot grigio. A little drier than the Riesling

but not as dry as the chardonnay you were considering." She reached for the bottle, but before she could make contact, Daniel had inserted his business card into her hand. She wheeled around to face him. "I'm trying to do my job here."

"And I'm trying to do mine." He pressed the card against her palm. "Please at least consider my offer."

"I don't think so." She took the card, tore it in half and let the pieces flutter to the floor. "I have no interest in anything you have to say to me. Not now, not ever. Go find someone else to torment." Then she turned back to her customer, exhaling only when she heard the shop's door close again.

CHAPTER TWO

A PINK blur came hurtling across the room and straight into Daniel's arms. "Daddy!"

He laughed and picked up his daughter, cradling her to his chest. Deep, fierce love bloomed inside him and he tightened his embrace, inhaling the strawberry scent of Annabelle's shampoo. There were days when he couldn't believe this four-year-old miracle was actually his.

A sharp pain ran through him as he thought of Sarah, and all she was missing. In the year since Sarah had died, it seemed like Annabelle had grown and changed in a hundred different ways. And his wife, the woman who had taken to motherhood as if she'd been made only for that single purpose, hadn't been here to see a single moment. Damn. Tears stung his eyes, but he blinked them back before Annabelle saw.

"Glad you're here. That girl about wore me out. She's a ball of energy. A cute ball." Greta Reynolds, Daniel's mother, reached out a hand and ruffled Annabelle's hair. "We played hide-and-seek, built an entire city with Barbie dolls, baked a batch of chocolate chip cookies and wore the colors off the Candy Land board."

Daniel hoisted Annabelle up a little higher. "Is that so?"

Annabelle nodded. "Uh-huh."

"Sounds like a fun day."

"It was. Now I have to get some dinner in the oven." Greta gave Daniel's shoulder a pat, then crossed to the kitchen counter where some chicken and a selection of vegetables waited to be assembled into something edible.

"Here, Daddy," Annabelle said, grabbing her father's hand and dragging him toward the kitchen table. "Come to my tea party."

He bit back a groan. Another tea party. A plastic tea set had been set up on the round maple surface, and two of the four chairs were occupied by Boo-Boo, her stuffed bear and a large pink rabbit whose name Daniel couldn't remember. Before he could say no, Annabelle had tugged him into a chair and climbed into the opposite one. He reached for a plastic cup, but Annabelle stopped him. "No, Daddy. You have to wear this." She flung a fluffy bright pink scarf at him.

He gave it a dubious look. "I have to *wear* this?"

Annabelle thrust out her lower lip. "Daddy, it's a *tea* party." As if that explained everything.

He'd done business lunches in five-star restaurants. Interviewed visiting dignitaries. Attended fancy black-tie dinners. One would think he could sit through a tea party with his daughter without wanting to run for the hills. But every time it came to pretending, or being silly, Daniel's sensible, logical side prevailed, and he became this stiff robot. He pushed the pink scarf to the side. "Uh, why don't you just pour the tea, Belle?"

She feigned pouring liquid into the tiny cup. "Here, Daddy."

He picked his up and tipped it to the side. "There's no tea in it."

"Daddy, you're s'posed to pretend." Annabelle let out another frustrated sigh. She picked up her cup, extended her pinkie and sipped at the invisible tea. "See?"

Annabelle's disappointment in him as a tea party attendee was clear in her tone and her face. He'd let his daughter down, the one thing he didn't want to do. But he felt out of his depth, as lost as a man in the desert without a compass, and every time he tried to correct his course, he seemed to make it worse. Hadn't that been a constant refrain from Sarah? He was never there, never around to bond, and now his absences were biting him back. "I'm sorry, honey. I'm just not very good at tea parties."

"No, you're not," Annabelle mumbled, and turned to her bear, tipping the cup toward his sewn-on mouth.

It had been easier interviewing the president of the United States than sitting here, pretending to drink tea. When it became clear that Annabelle wasn't going to invite him back to the party, Daniel got to his feet. A sense of defeat filled him. "Uh, I think Grandma needs me."

Daniel crossed to the counter, picked up a loaf of bread and began slicing it. A second later, he felt his mother's hand on his shoulder.

Greta turned toward Annabelle. "Honey, I think you forgot to invite Whitney to the tea party. You should go get her. I bet she's feeling lonely in your room."

"Oh, Whitney! You're right, Grandma!" Annabelle scrambled to her feet and dashed off down the hall.

Daniel chided himself. He hadn't even noticed Annabelle's favorite stuffed animal wasn't in attendance.

He was missing the details once again. For a man whose job had depended on details, he couldn't believe he could be so bad at it in his personal life.

"It'll get easier," Greta said, as if she'd read his mind.

He sighed. "I hope so."

"Thanks, Mom." He glanced at his mother, who looked about ready to collapse with exhaustion. But he saw the indulgent smiles she gave her only grandchild and knew Greta enjoyed every minute with energetic Annabelle. "For everything."

"Anytime."

He put the bread knife in the sink, then stood back while his mother bustled between stove and counter, assembling some kind of casserole. "How's she doing?"

"Okay." Greta paused in her mixing. "I don't think she quite understands that you've moved. To her, this has just been one long visit with Grandma."

"Eventually, I'm sure she'll settle in. It's been hard on her." Daniel thought of all the changes his daughter had been through in the past year. He hoped this was the last one. He needed to give her some stability, a proper house, a yard, heck, a puppy. Every child deserved that, and thus far, he hadn't done a very good job of delivering on any of the above. But here, in Winter Haven, he hoped he would find all of that. And he hoped he could make his career work here as well as he had in New York. Or at least work, period.

That was the only option possible. If he didn't, he'd have to take a job like the one he'd left—and that meant travel and long hours, two things a single father didn't need. His daughter needed him here as much as possible. If he'd learned anything at all in the past year, it was that.

His mother, sensing his thoughts, laid a hand on his shoulder. "You're doing fine, Daniel. She'll be okay."

He sighed, watching Annabelle bound across the kitchen, her pink dress swirling around her like a cloud. She looked so innocent, so carefree. So happy. Something he hadn't seen in a long time. Being here, with her indulgent grandmother, had been good for her. But still, he knew, there was a long road ahead of them. Whenever it was just him and Belle, things got tough again as both of them tried to dance around a subject neither wanted to tackle. And as he learned how to become a single dad to a girly daughter he barely understood. "I hope so."

"I know so." Greta patted his shoulder again. "I've raised a couple kids. So I get to claim expert status."

He reached up and squeezed his mother's hand. Greta had been a huge support over the past year. Flying up to New York and staying in those first difficult weeks while Daniel scrambled to bury his wife, figure out his life and figure out how he was going to raise Annabelle and keep his job. At first, he'd thought he could make it all work, but then the long hours and frequent trips his job as a newscaster demanded started to take their toll, and he realized it was time to make a change. The words Sarah had thrown at him, over and over again as their marriage disintegrated in the months before her death, finally took root.

He might not have been able to make his marriage work, but he would make this fatherhood thing work. That meant taking a position with nine-to-five hours, one that didn't leave Annabelle in day care from sunup to sundown, or leave her with the nanny while he jetted off to another country for an interview.

Which was what had brought him to the last thing

he wanted to do—produce "infotainment" shows that had about as much worth as frosting. His father was probably rolling over in his grave knowing Daniel was working for that show. Still, it was for his daughter. He kept that in mind with every step he took. With Greta's guiding hand, he hoped the transition would be easy on Annabelle. And him.

Beyond that—marrying again, having a life of his own—he couldn't think. Later, he told himself. Later.

"Annabelle, I think your father would like to try one of your cookies that we made today." Greta glanced at Daniel.

"Oh, yes, I would. Very much." Thank goodness for his mother. He'd already forgotten they'd baked cookies.

"Can I get two?" Annabelle asked, her hand hovering over the cooling treats. "One for me, and one for Daddy?"

Greta nodded, and Annabelle scooped up two chocolate chip cookies. "Here you go, Daddy." Annabelle held out a misshapen lump of cooked dough. "I made it all by myself."

"Looks delicious." He bit into the cookie, making a big deal out of the first bite. Annabelle beamed, so proud of the dessert she'd shaped with her own hands.

She wagged a finger at him. "You can only have one, Daddy, 'cuz we gotta eat dinner."

He gave her a solemn nod. "Okay, kiddo."

Annabelle's gaze dropped to the extra cookie in her hands. "I wish Mommy could have a cookie, too."

Her soft words broke Daniel's heart. The loss of her mother had hit Annabelle hard, and every so often, that pain slipped into the simplest of moments. He searched for the right words to say, and once again, came up empty. How could he begin to fill that yawning hole in Annabelle's heart when he was still trying to figure this out himself?

"I don't want my cookie anymore." The little girl's blue eyes filled with tears. The dessert tumbled from her hand onto the table.

"I have an idea," Greta said, bending down to her granddaughter's level. "Why don't we put this cookie next to your mommy's picture? Then when she looks down on us from heaven, she can see that you made her one, too."

"Will that make her happy?"

"I think so, sweetie." She took Annabelle's hand and they crossed to the long shelf that ran along the back wall of the kitchen. In the center, Annabelle's favorite picture of her mother sat, smiling down at them. Greta had placed it there the first day he and Annabelle had arrived, telling Belle it was so her mommy could watch over her every day. That time, and this one, his mother had stepped in with just the right touch, the one Daniel was still struggling to find.

Greta hoisted Belle into her arms, then let her put the cookie down just so. Then she hugged her tight, and when Belle's little arms wrapped around Greta's neck, Daniel's resolve to get close to his daughter again doubled. Somehow, he would find a way back for them.

Her mission accomplished, Annabelle ran off to play with her toys in the living room, leaving Daniel alone with his mother. Once she was sure Annabelle was out of earshot, Greta gestured toward the kitchen table. Daniel took a seat while his mother checked something simmering on the stove. "How's your first week at the new job going?"

"Well, it's a trial run. They want to see what I can

bring in for stories, and if they like what they see, I'll get a permanent position on the show. I hate this limbo. I just want to settle down again and know that tomorrow will be just like today. Not just for me, but for Belle, too."

"You will," Greta said. "You're a great reporter. Just like your father."

There were days—more of them in the past year—when that comparison grated. His father had been a legendary reporter, with a Pulitzer Prize to prove it. Before that, Daniel's grandfather had been a reporter, and probably in some distant caveman days, there was a Reynolds who had etched information onto a cave wall. "I *was* a great reporter, Mom. Then my life fell apart and I went from great to awful." He thought of the awards that had once hung proudly over his desk, then began to collect dust, then finally seemed to mock him and he'd put them in the bottom of a drawer.

"Nobody can blame you. You went through a terrible year—"

"Ratings don't care about personal problems, Mom. And once your ratings tank, so does your career." How many times had his father drummed that into his head? *It's all about ratings, son. Do what it takes to stay at the top.*

His mother bit her lower lip, as if she was holding back what she truly wanted to say. "So, tell me, what stories are you working on now?"

"I've got a couple who've been married sixty-three years and still go dancing together every Friday night, a dog who took care of a litter of kittens when the mother cat died." He ticked off the subjects on his fingers.

"Oh. Well, those are interesting." But everything in her voice said otherwise.

"And—" he grinned, saving his best prospect for last "—a real-life princess. Or at least, that's what she's claiming she is."

"A princess? Wait, you don't mean that one in Boston, do you? I don't remember her name, but I remember seeing her on the national news."

"Not her. Her sister. She's working at a wine shop downtown. She claims to be the youngest sister of the Uccelli princesses."

"And you think she's lying?"

"Well, it seems convenient that she's saying that when the other princess is halfway across the country. Not to mention this Carrie woman is working in some little shop in a tiny town in the Midwest. During tourist season." He thought of the woman he'd met today, how un-royal she seemed. Her long, dark hair, pulled back into a ponytail, the simple T-shirt, the near-perfect English. The way she'd laughed, so unreserved, so free. And she could talk wine well—as if she'd worked in a vineyard or a wine shop for years. Definitely not a job he'd ever heard a princess holding. Dignitary, lawyer, humanitarian, yes. Grape picker? No.

"Maybe she likes a quiet life. You don't get much quieter than this town." His mother laughed.

Carrie had been beautiful, in an understated, natural way. The kind of woman who looked even prettier without makeup than with. She'd intrigued him, but he wasn't sure if that was just professional curiosity or something more.

Either way, he had enough on his plate without adding something more.

"Uccelli...Uccelli." Greta thought a second. "You

know, there was a rumor around here years ago. Must be more than twenty years now. There was a woman—I don't remember her name now—who came here and stayed in one of the lake cottages for the summer. After she left, someone saw her on TV and said she looked just like the queen of Uccelli. For a while, that was all the gossip buzz around here. That the queen had taken a secret vacation in Winter Haven." Greta shrugged. "Could be a fairy tale. You know how people like to think they can see Mickey Mouse in their morning toast."

Daniel chuckled. "I do."

"If the queen story is true, then maybe her daughter is just following in her footsteps."

"Maybe. I don't know much about princesses," he said, "but she seemed as far removed from being one as you could get."

"Well, maybe it is a marketing gimmick. Or maybe—" his mother laid a hand on his shoulder "—you're too jaded to see the truth."

"Doesn't matter," Daniel said. Maybe yes, he was jaded. But it was easier to be that way than to let every emotion he saw into his heart. Much easier to be steel than putty. "Either way, I'm going to ferret out the truth. I have a feeling this story is the one that can launch my career at *Inside Scoop,* and one way or another, I'm running with it."

Carrie rubbed her neck, then stretched her back and shoulders. The shop had been impossibly busy today, and every muscle in her body ached. But it was a good ache, the kind that came from a job well done. She could hardly wait to see the week's end numbers. It all boded well for the future of Uccelli's wines in

America. And that, in turn, boded well for her future as a vineyard owner.

She flipped the sign to Closed and breathed a sigh of relief that the TV reporter from the other day hadn't been back. She didn't need that distraction interfering with her plans. She had a limited window of time and a lot to learn and accomplish during that period. She wanted to get more involved on the retail end, taking the time to study the bookkeeping, the ordering process, the sales trends. The last thing she needed was a member of the paparazzi looking for a scandal to exploit.

"I think we're going to need to hire more help at this rate," Faith said as she pulled the last outdoor display into the shop for the night. "I've never seen this place so busy." She patted Carrie on the back. "Thanks to the princess here."

"I'm just glad to help."

"Whatever you're doing, keep on doing it, because it's working." Faith shrugged on a light jacket, then grabbed her purse. "I'll see you Monday."

"Monday?"

"We're closed Sundays. Which means you, my friend, get a day off." Faith let out a long breath that said she was just as exhausted as Carrie. "And thank goodness, so do I."

A few minutes later, Faith and Carrie had finished locking up the shop, and they headed their separate ways. The long night—and next day—stretched ahead of Carrie with no plans. She couldn't think of the last time her time had truly been her own, something she could fill any way she liked with no worries that someone was expecting her to be somewhere else, no guilt that she was ducking an obligation. Castle life was busy, with events piled on top of more events, with at least one representative of the royal family expected to be in attendance at all times. When she hadn't been working in the vineyard, she'd been forced into donning stiff suits or ruffled gowns and pasting a smile on her face for the few royal events she couldn't wrangle a way out of. Even in the castle, there'd always been maids underfoot, and people in and out all day and night.

And now she had a whole blissful day and a half? Totally, utterly alone?

Carrie started to drive toward her lake house, then saw a sign for the Winter Haven Library. Soft golden light still glowed in the small brick building's windows and drew her like a beacon.

How long had it been since she'd been able to sit down and read an entire book from start to finish? Enjoy the story without interruptions from staff, visitors, events? The thought of doing something as decadent as just reading filled her with a warm sense of anticipation. She parked, then stepped inside the building and inhaled the slightly musty, slightly dusty scent of lots and lots of books. She'd hated boarding school—hated the boring classes, the endless rules, but most of all, hated being away from the wild land that surrounded Uccelli's castle—but she had loved the library at St. Mary's. It had been massive, and filled with every book one could imagine, and had made the boarding school experience more tolerable for a girl who would have rather been home in her beloved vineyards than memorizing algebraic equations. She'd spent her free moments curled up in a comfortable chair, lost in worlds completely unlike her own.

That's what she needed now. A good book, something

she could take back to that little nook in the lake house and enjoy with a cup of hot tea while the soft breezes from the water whispered around her. The prospect hurried her steps, and she headed into the first book-filled room she saw.

Almost immediately she realized she'd entered the children's section by mistake. She started to turn around when she heard a male voice, a familiar low baritone. "Just one more book, Belle. Then we need to get home."

"Daddy, I wanna read a princess story."

A sigh. "What about this one? It's about George Washington growing up."

A matching sigh from much younger lungs. "No. I don't want that one. It's yucky. Read me a *princess* story."

Carrie grinned. She recognized that stubborn streak and had heard that defiance in herself. Carrie took a couple steps forward and peeked around the bookshelf. Her gaze lighted first on a little girl with a headful of blond curls spilling around her shoulders like a halo. She had on a ruffled pink-and-white dress and plastic glittery shoes with a tiny heel. She had her little fists perched on her hips and was glaring at the man before her—

Oh, no.

A very exasperated-looking Daniel Reynolds. Carrie jerked back, but not fast enough. "Annabelle…" Daniel's voice trailed off when he glanced up and noticed Carrie standing there.

"I'm…I'm sorry," she said. Was she stammering? She never stammered. "I, uh, walked into the children's area by mistake. I didn't expect to see…well, see you here."

His chiseled features met hers with a direct, intent stare. No surprise, just…assessment. "Nor did I expect to see you."

"I'll…I'll leave you to your book."

"It's her!"

The voice behind Carrie startled her and she spun around to find one of her customers from earlier that day. The woman stepped forward, tugging her husband with her. "You're the princess, aren't you? The one from the wine shop?"

Carrie nodded and bit back a smile. People got such a chuckle out of her royal status. Carrie, who had lived as much out of the castle's shadow as she could, found the whole thing amusing.

The woman yanked on her husband's arm. "See, I told you she was here in Winter Haven. A real, honest-to-goodness princess."

The little girl with Daniel stared up at Carrie, her blue eyes wide and curious. "You're a *princess?* A real one?"

Carrie bent down slightly. "I am."

The little girl's mouth opened into a tiny O. "Wow." She tilted her head and gave Carrie a curious look. "Where's your crown?"

"Back home in Uccelli, where I come from."

"But don't princesses always have to wear a crown so everybody knows they're special?"

"Princesses are special every day, Annabelle." Carrie gave the girl a smile, then turned to her customer. "It's nice to see you again."

"You, too." The woman beamed. "We come to Winter Haven every summer for vacation. Have been for more than twenty years. I meant to tell you that I met your mother years ago."

"You did?"

"Uh-huh. She was telling people she was just an ordinary vacationer, but we knew better, didn't we?" She elbowed her husband, who grunted a yes. "She loved this place."

"She did, indeed," Carrie said.

"I don't blame her." The woman let out a little chuckle and winked. "Maybe you'll have the same amount of fun."

Carrie smiled. "Maybe." She exchanged a little bit of small talk before the woman and her husband left, promising to stop at By the Glass again before their vacation ended.

"Well, well," Daniel said after the couple left the room. "Seems the princess angle is good for sales."

She bristled. "That isn't why I told people who I am."

He arched a brow. "It isn't?"

"Of course not." She glared at him. "You always see the worst in people, don't you?"

"Why would you say that?"

"Because you people are jaded and bitter and think everyone is lying."

His face hardened and she knew she'd struck a nerve. "Well, perhaps if people didn't tell us lies all the time, reporters wouldn't be so jaded."

"I'm not—"

"Here, read this one." The little girl thrust a book between them. Then she leaned in closer to her father and lowered her voice. "And Daddy, you're not supposed to fight with a princess."

The lines in Daniel's face softened, and the hard edge disappeared. He bent down to his daughter's level and took the book from her hands. "You're right, Belle."

She beamed, then spun on those plastic pink shoes and thrust out a hand toward Carrie. "I'm Annabelle. I'm not a princess, but I wanna be one really bad."

Carrie laughed and shook the little girl's hand. Five fingers, so delicate, so soft and so reminiscent of herself and her sisters. "I'm Carlita Santaro, but you can call me Carrie."

"Princess Carrie." Annabelle glanced up at Carrie, all smiles and apple cheeks. "I like that name."

"Me, too." Carrie glanced at Daniel. He'd tamed his go-for-the-jugular reporter side for now. But how long would that last? In the end, she knew where his type gravitated—to the story. Regardless of the consequences or fallout. But a part of her wanted to know if a guy who could look at his daughter with such love in his eyes could be different. Still, her instincts told her to keep her distance. "I should go."

"Stay," Annabelle said. "'Cuz, Daddy's going to read a story and he's really good at reading stories."

"Oh, I don't think I should—"

But the little girl had already grabbed Carrie's hand and was tugging her in Daniel's direction. "You can sit over there. I can sit over here. And Daddy—" the girl stopped in front of her father, propped one fist on her hip, and gave him a stern look "—you can read."

Daniel let out a laugh, then sent Carrie an apologetic smile. "I'm sorry. Annabelle can be…demanding."

"Daddy! I'm not 'manding. I'm nice."

He chuckled again. "Yes, Belle, you are nice. The nicest little girl in the world."

Annabelle beamed and the love between father and daughter seemed to fill the small colorful space.

This other side of Daniel Reynolds surprised Carrie, but she refused to soften her stance on an interview about herself. She'd seen a hundred times how trusting someone from the media could turn around and bite her. Hadn't they been painting her as the "extra" princess for years? As if the royal family could discard her because she'd never be queen.

How did she know this guy wouldn't do the same? Or worse, just make something up?

No, if she allowed him into her world, it would be to talk about Uccelli's wines. And nothing more. And all the while she'd be wary, and not trust him.

But as she watched him interact with his daughter, a part of her wanted to believe he was different. That she could trust him.

"Come on," Annabelle said, tugging on Carrie's hand again. "You gotta sit down or Daddy won't read. It's a…" She glanced at her father for the word.

"Rule," Daniel supplied. Then he shrugged and smiled again. "Sorry, but it is."

Carrie thought of leaving. Then she caught Daniel's smile again, and something about it hit her square in the gut. He had a lopsided smile, the kind that gave his face character and depth, and had her following Annabelle to the square of carpet on Daniel's right. As soon as Carrie lowered herself onto the small space, Annabelle scrambled over to his opposite side, plunked down on her bottom and plopped her chin into her hands. "Read my story, Daddy."

He arched a brow.

"Please."

"Okay." He turned the cover of the book and then shot Carrie a glance. "Seems Belle has picked *The Princess and the Pea.* You know, the fairy tale about the woman they suspect is masquerading as a princess."

"I love that story," Annabelle said, completely oblivious to the hidden conversation between the adults. "'Cuz it's got a princess in it. I love princesses."

"Then by all means, I think you should read it," Carrie said to Daniel.

"I think I should, too. Refresh my memory." He leaned back against a beanbag chair, and Annabelle curled up next to him, laying her blond head on his chest so she could see the pictures as he read.

The father-daughter picture before her filled Carrie with a rush of sentiment. On the rare occasions when her mother had been home at night and around at bedtime, she'd made it a rule to read the girls at least one story, sometimes two. Always a fairy tale, because she said those were the kind of stories that taught you to dream. Carrie leaned against the bookcase, as enthralled as the little girl in Daniel's arms.

She'd stay just a minute, no more, and only because Annabelle had asked her. She didn't want to intrude. Or get any closer to this man.

"'Then she took twenty mattresses and laid them on top of the pea,'" Daniel read, his quiet voice seeming to spin a magical web, "'and then twenty eiderdown beds on top of the mattresses.'"

"Twenty?" Annabelle asked and fluttered her fingers as if she was counting that high. "That's lots."

"It is indeed," Daniel said, then turned another page. "'On this the princess had to lie all night. In the morning she was asked how she had slept.'" He paused. "What do you think, pumpkin? Was she a princess after all or another imposter?"

"What's a 'poster?"

"Well, Belle, that's a person who pretends to be something they're not." He closed the book, glanced at Carrie and arched a brow. "Would you agree, Miss Santaro?"

"I think lots of people pretend to be something they aren't."

"You have a point," he said. Their gazes met and for a moment, it felt like détente. Like they were starting something. What, Carrie wasn't sure.

"Daddy, you gotta read. I wanna know if the princess lives happy ever after. And so does Princess Carrie."

Daniel glanced at Carrie and arched a brow. A teasing grin darted across his face. Was he…flirting with her? Or merely playing into Annabelle's game? "Well, Princess Carrie? Do you want me to keep reading?"

She waved toward the book. "Please do, Mr. Reynolds. I'm dying to hear how this one ends."

His gaze met hers and something hot pooled inside her. "I am, too," he said. Then he opened the book again and began to read.

CHAPTER THREE

"Okay, new guy, what have you got?"

At the sound of his boss's voice, Daniel jerked to attention in his chair. He faced Matt Harrod and the rest of the production team, a motley crew of producers, cameramen and the two hosts who provided commentary for *Inside Scoop,* all gathered for a quick Saturday-morning meeting. Daniel was the only one with a hard news background, and in the few days that he had been working here, he'd begun to feel like he was living on an alien planet. Everyone at *Inside Scoop* wanted the next sensational spot, the next media meltdown. They were like vultures hovering over a steaming carcass of scandal. Daniel missed the days when he produced stories that had meaning, the kind that brought viewers an important message or changed a life. The kind that his father had done, the kind that were part of the Reynolds family legacy.

But those stories came with a job that demanded long hours, frequent and last-minute trips around the world, and a daughter who was raised by strangers. Daniel told himself the job he had now was perfect, and he better start acting like it.

"I found a princess…or rather, someone who claims

to be a princess," he said to Matt, "living temporarily in Winter Haven."

Matt let out a gust of disbelief. "Like real, honest-to-God royalty?"

"Seems it, though I'm still researching her." He pulled his notes before him. "This woman, Carlita Santaro, is claiming she's the third daughter of the king of Uccelli, a country near Italy. I checked, and there is a real Carlita who fits the age and looks similar. Her middle sister, Allegra, ascended to the throne last year, and her oldest sister, Mariabella, is married to an American and spends part of her time running an art gallery in Massachusetts. Her mother spent time here more than twenty years ago, which is what Carlita says drew her to this town."

"I think I heard about the art chick. She was in the news last year. Wish I'd gotten that scoop." Matt made a few notes on a pad of paper. "So what's number three doing in Indiana?"

"Her country makes wine. And she's running a small wine shop that is the first in the United States to sell Uccelli wines. Sort of a test market with the tourists."

"You sure she's the real deal?" Matt asked.

Daniel shrugged. "So far, her story checks out."

"So far?" Matt arched a brow. The rest of the production team turned toward Daniel.

"Well, there's not much information on Carlita Santaro." He opened the folder before him and withdrew the few pictures he had of Carrie in her royal element. He scattered them across the long conference table while he spoke. "Partly because she has always shunned the spotlight and partly because she's the third daughter, and thus not as interesting to the media. So it's been a bit of a challenge proving this Carlita's story."

Matt picked up one of Carrie's headshots, this one a few years old and a little grainy. "Did you run a blood test?"

Daniel chuckled. "Seriously? I can't do that."

"Seriously. I don't want to put this station on the line for some half-baked crazy who thinks she's the latest Romanov descendent."

Daniel bristled, and forced himself to tamp down his anger. This was his job here—his first chance to prove himself to his new boss—and he needed to stay in control. Good paying media jobs in the middle of the country weren't exactly plentiful, and if he didn't succeed at this one, he'd be forced to move back to the coast and put Annabelle back into the same nanny/day care/absent father nightmare he had worked so hard to leave behind. That was assuming he could find another job in the news, considering how his reputation had fallen apart last year. He'd applied to twenty places with no luck before he'd been hired here. He needed this job, as much as he hated that his options had narrowed to this. "The stories I read about her fit the woman that I met. I'm not a hundred percent positive she's the real princess yet. I still need to do a bit more legwork to make sure."

Matt considered the information for a while, twirling his pen between his fingers as he thought. His face was filled with skepticism, and the trademark scheming that had helped his show rise in the ratings. Whatever he was thinking, Daniel was pretty damned sure it was going to be some harebrained idea, and undoubtedly something Daniel wouldn't like. In the two weeks Daniel had been working here, he'd watched

Matt cross the journalism line a hundred times. In fact, Daniel wouldn't call much of what Matt did *journalism.*

Daniel had met interns out of college with more tact and experience. But this was the job he had, and that meant he had to buck up and tolerate Matt's insensitive personality. For now. Soon as he had a success back on his résumé, Daniel was heading for a job that had more meat than sugar.

"All right, we'll give it a shot," Matt said. "But I don't want to do the typical profile piece." He mocked a yawn. "We need something that will put us on the map. The kind of piece that the other stations will want to run on their shows. Something that really puts *Inside Scoop* into the public eye. I want to go global, baby, and this is the kind of story that can help us do that. World, here we come!"

"Okay," Daniel said. "I'll think of an angle that—"

"I don't want an angle. I want something that says *wow.* Something like…" He twirled the pen some more, and then his face brightened in a way that Daniel knew meant something bad was coming out of Matt's mouth. "A test."

"A test?"

"Yeah, like that fairy tale. What is the name of it again?" He smacked the arm of the young male intern beside him. The kid—no older than twenty—jumped.

"Uh…*Cinderella?*" he said in a squeaky voice.

"No, no, the other one."

"Snow White," Emily, the female half of the cohost team, volunteered.

"No. God. I work with a bunch of idiots." Matt cursed. "What the hell is the name of that fairy tale?

The one where they test the princess. Make sure she's Grade A."

"The Princess and the Pea," Daniel said, then hated himself for supplying the answer. He could already see the road ahead and he didn't like the direction Matt was traveling. As much as anyone, he wanted to prove—or disprove—Carrie's claim, but not in some sensationalized circus.

"Yes! That's it!" Matt pointed at Daniel and beamed. "New guy, you just earned your keep. I think you've got the best story idea out of all these idiots. You run with your princess and get a little background on her. We'll work on developing the test to prove she's royalty."

"What possible test could there be?"

Matt grinned, the kind of grin that Daniel knew meant this was going in the wrong direction. Dread filled the pit of Daniel's stomach and he wondered if it was too late to retract the story.

"Oh, we'll think of something," Matt said. "But whatever we think of, I can guarantee one thing."

"What's that?" Daniel asked.

"It'll be great TV." Matt grinned. "Great, memorable, big bucks TV."

"That's what I'm afraid of," Daniel muttered as he gathered his things and left the production meeting. And tried like hell to think of a way to tell Carrie about this without her wanting to shove that tiara down his throat.

Annabelle skipped in a circle around the kitchen. She had on her plastic tiara and a purple dress that blossomed out from her waist in a wide bell. He'd tried like hell to talk her out of the tiara, but Annabelle had insisted, and Daniel hadn't wanted to see a frown on his little girl's face. Not when she'd just started smiling again.

"You ready, pumpkin?"

She stopped twirling and turned to face him. "Uh-huh."

She'd been ready and waiting when he got home from the production meeting. Now her excitement shimmered on her face, danced in her eyes. "All right then, let's go." He put out his hand for Annabelle. She started toward him, then stopped and grabbed a bright pink bag sitting on the kitchen table. "What's that?"

"I can't tell you, Daddy. It's a s'prise." An impish grin spread across her pixie features.

"A surprise, huh?" He bent down and pretended to try to peek inside the bag. "For me?"

She jerked the silky bag away. "No peeking, Daddy! It's not for you."

"For Grandma?"

"No, silly. For the princess." Annabelle beamed and clutched the bag to her chest. "We're gonna be princesses together today."

Daniel bit back a groan. He wished Annabelle hadn't found out about Carrie's identity. But she'd been right there, her four-year-old teapot ears listening in when the library patron had stopped in the children's department and exclaimed over finding Winter Haven's resident "princess" in such an ordinary place. Annabelle had been awed and excited, and before Daniel could stop her, she'd been inviting Carrie along on the father-daughter picnic in the park that Daniel had planned for today.

At first, he'd resisted the idea, then he realized a picnic was the perfect opportunity to get to know

Carrie and to find out if she was the real Carlita Santaro or an imposter. Before he went much further at *Inside Scoop* with the story, he wanted to be sure one way or another. Matt's test was one method, but Daniel preferred to do things the old-fashioned way. Digging up facts, assembling them, until he got the truth.

And right now, he wasn't sure what the truth was concerning the "princess" working the wine shop counter.

In the pictures of the royal family he'd found, Princess Carlita was either not there or far in the background. Convenient, he figured, for someone who wanted to take Carlita Santaro's place halfway around the world in a tiny tourist town in Indiana most people had never heard of. Was she here to capitalize on the rumored visit of the queen of Uccelli, more than two decades ago? There'd been little media coverage of Bianca Santaro's visit—just a few speculating pieces in European papers and a tidbit in the Indianapolis paper—nothing really confirmed. But definitely something he'd spend a little more time researching. Either way, for all intents and purposes, the queen of Uccelli had entered and exited the town while remaining anonymous. Perhaps her daughter wanted to retrace her mother's visit?

The photographed Carlita had curled hair swept up into some elaborate hairdo, her dresses so bejeweled they looked like they weighed a hundred pounds. Not the girl-next-door he'd met a couple days ago. Yet, the official quotes from the palace about the "shy" princess contrasted with several media reports about some "adventures," as the Uccelli media dubbed them. Whichever the case—quiet girl or wild child— it seemed the real Carlita Santaro had shunned the spotlight and done her best to shun her royal life, too. Could the smiling, outgoing woman he'd met be the same one who'd ditched a state dinner, commandeered a castle vehicle and headed into the countryside for a two-day camping adventure with her friends?

Either way, he needed more information before he put her on the air. With any luck, this story would be the blockbuster he was looking for and become the kind of thing that netted him a permanent position in Indiana. It wasn't the glamorous globe-trotting career he'd once had or even the meaty reporter work he'd built his career upon, and far removed from the gritty, Pulitzer-winning journalism of his father and grandfather, but it was the perfect job for a single father who needed a reboot on his life. And to earn a way back into the journalism elite.

The best way to get an interview subject to talk, he'd found, was to bring them to a casual setting and hope they relaxed enough to spill their guts. A picnic, he'd decided after Annabelle proposed the idea, would be the perfect place. He had gathered enough information on Uccelli and the royal family that he hoped after today's fact-finding mission, he could either reveal Carrie as a fraud or prove her identity.

And yes, a part of him was intrigued by this woman with a slight accent and a wide smile. Intrigued on a level that had nothing to do with the story.

He hadn't been intrigued by a woman in a long time. After the car accident that took Sarah's life, he'd wanted nothing more than to be alone. To drop out of the world. He couldn't, because he had Belle, but there were a lot of days when just getting out of bed was hell. He hadn't thought about dating—much less marrying—again. Although his marriage had been over except for the signing of the divorce papers before Sarah's accident, considering another relationship hadn't even been on his radar.

And now this woman, a stranger really, had sent his mind spiraling down a path he'd considered sealed.

A path he had no intentions of taking again. Hadn't he already done it wrong once before? Nearly losing his relationship with his daughter in the process? No, he decided. Work only. Relationships could wait.

His mother came into the living room and thrust a small red cooler into Daniel's hands. "I packed sandwiches, a few bottles of water and some of Annabelle's cookies."

"I could have done that, Mom."

She laughed. "You would have forgotten the napkins. And the water bottles. Not to mention your sandwiches would have been some god-awful meat combination."

He grinned. "Probably. I'm not very domesticated, I guess."

"You're trying. That's enough."

He let out a gust and thought of last night, when he'd tried to put Annabelle to bed. His daughter had resisted, whining and complaining and pitching such a tantrum that his mother had finally come in and soothed the waters. There were days when Daniel felt like he had no idea how to connect with his own child. What kind of father did that make him?

"Besides, maybe I like taking care of my son and granddaughter." Greta gave him a tender smile.

He leaned over and pressed a soft kiss to her cheek. His mother had done so much in the past year, and he wondered if he could ever begin to thank her. His gratitude that he and Greta had found their way back to a close mother-son relationship filled his chest. "Thank you."

"Daddy, come on!" Annabelle tugged on the sleeve of his button-down shirt. "We're gonna be late for the *princess*."

His mother smiled. "Better hurry. You don't want to keep a princess waiting."

"Even pseudo ones," he muttered.

"Daddy, what's soo-do?" Annabelle asked.

He scowled. His daughter heard everything—except words like *clean up your toys* or *go to sleep.* "It just means I want to ask her all about being a princess."

"Me, too," Annabelle said. "I wanna know *everything.*"

But as they walked out the door, Daniel knew the answers he and his daughter were seeking were very, very different.

Carrie had changed her outfit three times before she finally got mad at her reflection and told herself this wasn't a date. She was going on a picnic, and going with Daniel Reynolds only because Daniel's daughter had heard the word *princess* and been instantly enchanted. There was no way Carrie could say no to those earnest, wide blue eyes and Annabelle's *please-please-please.* Unlike her father, Annabelle Reynolds was adorable and charming, the kind of child who could melt even the coldest heart.

Had Daniel agreed to the picnic as a way of pumping Carrie for information? Or because he was genuinely interested in Carrie Santaro, the person? Only one way to find out, she decided, and that was to go.

Still, she hesitated. She knew better than to trust him. A part of her, the part that had spent all her life not knowing if the people she met were true friends or merely looking to rub elbows with a royal, wondered about Daniel's intentions.

Trust. A lot of meaning in five little letters.

Carrie glanced at the clock. She'd better hurry or she'd be late. She settled on a pale yellow dress with a cotillion of white flowers dancing around the skirt. She paired it with white flats and a short white sweater. It certainly wasn't one of the fancy dresses or stiff suits she wore for royal appearances. This dress—something she had bought in a shop in downtown Winter Haven a few days ago—definitely better suited Carrie's keep-it-simple philosophy. She kept her hair simple, too, leaving it down and slightly wavy around her shoulders.

Then she packed a small container with some cheese, crackers and fresh grapes and put everything into a cloth tote. At the last second, she grabbed a bottle of her favorite Uccelli wine and added it to the tote bag. If Daniel tried to turn this into a life-as-a-princess interview, she'd change the subject to the one that really interested her. She had no intentions of letting him exploit her for his news program. She was there for Annabelle, nothing more.

She walked the three blocks to the park, enjoying the warm day, cooled by a gentle breeze. If she closed her eyes, she could almost believe she was back walking the rocky shores of Uccelli while the gulls shrieked warnings and the terns danced in the surf. Except the air here lacked the tangy saltwater scent, and gulls were a rare sighting.

The Winter Haven Town Park wasn't very big, as parks went. A large gazebo with gingerbread-patterned trim anchored the park in the middle, while a bright-colored playground took up the eastern corner. A small pond held court on the western side, flanked by a half dozen picnic tables. Canada geese milled about the pond, picking at the grass and searching for stray bread crumbs. Children laughed while they climbed the jungle gym and their parents hovered nearby, ready to prevent a fall or a bruise.

Everything here was so simple, so ordinary. Carrie loved the homespun nature of this small town, the way everyone seemed to know everyone else. No wonder her mother had loved it so much. A tiny whisper sounded in the back of Carrie's mind. If Bianca had loved this town so much, why had she been so resistant to Carrie coming here herself?

Yet the tourist trade was brisk, people drawn by both the beautiful, expansive lake and the friendly, bucolic atmosphere. Instead of hotels, the town had a varied selection of bed-and-breakfasts. It was almost like being at home.

After only a week here, she could walk into nearly any store in Winter Haven and people greeted her by name. The residents didn't see her as Princess Carlita, they saw only Carrie.

It was the most liberating experience of Carrie's life. No wonder Mama had loved it so much.

Carrie strode down the paved path and rounded the corner of the twenty-foot-tall wooden gazebo. There, standing by the pond, was Daniel Reynolds and his daughter. Carrie bit back a laugh at the little girl's fluffy purple dress and the rhinestone tiara sparkling in her golden curls. All little girls wanted to be princesses—except the ones who actually were royal.

As Carrie approached, Annabelle turned and spied her. She dashed up the hill, waving her arms, her hair a wild cloud around her head, and jerked to a stop, teetering on her plastic heels. "Hi." She dipped her head, a shy smile curving across her face.

Carrie laughed. All that and one word. Carrie bent down to Annabelle's level. "Hi yourself, Annabelle. I like your crown."

Annabelle beamed, and her fingers fluttered over the delicate silver plastic arches of her tiara. "Thank you."

"I like your shoes, too."

"Thank you. They're my stick shoes." Annabelle held out a foot for Carrie to see the tiny heel. Then she screwed up her face and stared up at Carrie. "Where's your castle? Is your daddy the king? Did you get kissed by a prince?"

Daniel stopped beside his daughter and ruffled her hair. "Goodness, you're the girl of questions, little Belle."

Annabelle squinted irritation at her father. "But Daddy, I gotta know. I'll never be a princess if I don't know how."

Carrie pressed a quick touch to Annabelle's button nose. "You, sweetie, are already a princess."

Annabelle's bright smile rivaled the sun. "I am?"

"Uh-huh. Being a princess isn't about being royal or being the daughter of the king or being kissed by a prince. It's about being a good person, one who stands up for other people and takes care of them. A person who always stands up for what's important to her."

Annabelle wrinkled her nose, thinking. "I take care of Whitney. I do a real good job with her."

"Whitney is Belle's stuffed dog," Daniel supplied. "She's had her since she was a baby."

Annabelle frowned. "Daddy, I'm not a baby."

"I know, pumpkin, I know." He chuckled, then

gestured down the hill. "Annabelle and I set up quite the spread under that maple tree, if you'd like to join us."

"I'd love to."

Annabelle squealed with delight, then grabbed Carrie's hand and practically dragged her down the hill to a red plaid blanket. An open cooler sat in one corner, and a stuffed animal sat in the other. Carrie dropped onto the blanket beside Annabelle and picked up the dog. "Is this Whitney?"

Annabelle nodded. "She loves picnics."

"Me, too, Whitney," Carrie said to the dog. "Nice to meet another picnic fan." She handed the tan dog over to Annabelle, who clutched it to her chest in a tight hug.

"Princesses have picnics?" Annabelle asked.

"Not very often," Carrie said, then thought of the last time she'd enjoyed something like this. She'd been ten, and had escaped the castle when her mother wasn't looking, ditching the stuffy state luncheon she'd been expected to attend. Still clad in her floor-length satin dress, she'd run barefoot to the vineyards and had a wonderful hour eating lunch with the workers sitting on the grassy knoll overlooking the vines. By the time Tavo, the manager of the vineyard, was handing out cookies for dessert, the worried staff had found Carrie and brought her back to the castle. She'd kept her cookie clutched tight in her hand, but it was just a pile of crumbs when she crossed the threshold of the castle. "Not nearly often enough," she added softly.

Daniel sat down across from them and withdrew a stack of paper plates and several thick ham-and-cheese sandwiches from the cooler. He placed a bottle of sparkling water on the blanket, then flanked it with plastic

cups and napkins. Carrie pulled her container out of
her bag, removed the lid, then placed the cheese and
crackers beside the sandwiches. Seemed this was going
to be just a picnic. Good.

Except a part of her was noticing Daniel's blue eyes,
the way his dark hair curled across his brow. Noticing
very, very much.

"You didn't have to bring anything," he said.

"One thing my mother insisted on was that I never
arrive empty-handed to an event. Even a princess
should be a gracious guest, she'd say. So I brought
grapes and cheese." She reached into the bag, and
pulled out the plastic containers, followed by the bottle
of wine. She showed it to him, then let it slide back into
the bag for now. "And a gift for the hostess, or in your
case, host. Though I have to say, you've outdone me."

He shook his head, and for a second, Carrie thought
Daniel Reynolds looked a bit embarrassed. "I have to
give my mother the credit for that. I can barely make a
PB and J for Belle."

"PB and J?" Carrie asked.

"Peanut butter and jelly," Annabelle said, then
pulled another sandwich out of the cooler, one filled
with the aforementioned ingredients. "It's the yummi-
est sammwich ever. Here, try." Annabelle yanked the
sandwich out of the clear plastic bag, sending a large
squirt of jelly spraying onto Carrie's skirt. It landed
with a thick thud, and seeped purple juices into the
pale yellow fabric.

Annabelle's eyes widened. "Oh, no. I'm sorry,
Princess Carrie. I'm sorry, sorry, sorry."

Carrie laughed and reached for a napkin to wipe off
the worst of it. "Believe me, it's okay. It's just jelly."

"But I made your princess dress messy." Annabelle pouted. "Sorry."

Carrie laid a hand on Annabelle's arm. A light, quick touch. "It's okay, Annabelle. Even princesses get dirty sometimes."

"Really?"

"Really." That was part of the appeal of working in the vineyards—she could get dirty, sweaty even, and no one cared. It was probably why Carrie had always been into hands-on activities. For a while, she'd ridden horses, then found it more fun to help in the stables. There'd been times she'd joined the landscapers in setting out annuals, other times when she'd headed for the vineyards for harvest time.

"When I'm in the castle," she said to Annabelle, "I have to look perfect all the time. Every hair, every thread in its place. There are always attendants, which are like helpers, hovering nearby, ready to fluff and nitpick. It did make me crazy, I have to say."

"Really?" a wide-eyed Annabelle said.

"Yes. And sometimes, all I wanted to do was run off to my room and change into jeans and flip-flops like other girls my age."

When she'd planned the trip to Winter Haven, she'd gone on an all-day shopping spree and filled her suitcase with nothing smacking of royalty. She glanced down at the purple blotch and hoped in a weird way that it never washed away.

Daniel was regarding her with a curious glance. She couldn't decide if it was interest or distrust. "You sure you don't want to go home and change?" he asked. "In case another reporter comes by or something? Being covered in jelly and at a picnic in the park is the kind of thing they love to splash on the front pages."

All her life, her parents had done their level best to keep the media's focus off Carrie's wild antics. Since she was the "spare" heir, their attention had usually been on Carrie's older sisters anyway. As a result, the media had painted her as the third daughter who lived in the shadows of the two elder bright stars of Mariabella and Allegra, with a few blips about her antics off castle grounds.

No more of that, Carrie decided. She was going to make her mark on the world. As herself, not as a princess.

She smiled, then reached forward, swiped another glob of jelly off the edge of the sandwich and smeared it along the edge of her skirt. "Let them," she said. "Because I'm not the princess they think I am."

CHAPTER FOUR

NOT the princess they thought she was. Daniel sat back on the blanket and regarded Carrie. That was a curious turn of phrase. Was she outright admitting she wasn't the real Carlita Santaro?

He decided not to press the issue. If he did, she might clam up and then he'd never get the information he needed. Instead, he handed out the ham-and-cheese sandwiches, poured the water and waited. Biding his time, he decided, was the best course of action. Because right now, Annabelle was making a hell of an interrogator.

The problem? He was having a hell of a time concentrating. Every time Carrie smiled, he wanted to make her smile again. He was supposed to be objective, to keep a clear head, and he kept on getting distracted by the little dimple winking with every smile. He found himself watching her mouth as she talked, wondering what it would be like to kiss her. If she would taste as sweet as she looked, if she would curve into his arms, or push him away.

He shook off the thoughts. He didn't need a relationship right now. Maybe not ever.

Annabelle gobbled her sandwich and ran off toward

the swing sets. In seconds, she was swinging back and forth, singing a song about princesses.

"Your daughter is adorable. And quite the character," Carrie said, laughing.

She had a light, lyrical laugh. Almost like a song, he thought. Damn, he kept getting distracted when he really needed to focus.

"Yes, she is." Daniel cleared his throat. "You must miss castle life."

Carrie's gaze went to something distant. Because she was carefully concocting her answer? Or because what he'd said had bothered her? "No, I really don't. I was never cut out for the royal thing."

"What makes you say that?"

She splayed one hand across the pale yellow skirt of her dress and brushed at imaginary lint. For whatever reason, she was delaying her answer. The cynic in him said it was because she was working on a lie. The intrigued man in him wondered if even princesses tired of their life of luxury.

He could relate to the grinding yoke of expectations. Hadn't he been expected to follow in the steps of his grandfather and father? They'd come attached to his name, to everything he did. There were times when he wondered what his life would have been like if he'd been a landscaper or an artist.

But the woman across from him, sitting so composed and serene, had a regal way about her. It was as if it was in her bones, part of her blood. Even though she was at a picnic, sitting on a blanket under a tree with jelly on her skirt.

"I'm not princess material," she said after a long while. "Though I tried really hard to be."

For a second, his heart went out to her. He knew

what it was like to try to live up to expectations that kept rising. To try to achieve an impossible goal. Wasn't that what working in television was all about? Always trying to top what had come before? And on top of that, being part of the Reynolds legacy.

Did she understand that, or was this all part of an elaborate ruse? His instincts said she was real, but his instincts had gotten fuzzy in the last year.

"So your mother vacationed here before," he said, leading into but not quite asking a question.

Carrie nodded. "It was before I was born. My sisters had gone on a vacation with my grandparents, a couple weeks on the Amalfi Coast, and my mother decided to take a vacation of her own."

"Did she do that a lot?"

"Not at all. Palace life is one of those all-consuming things. I think she spied her chance at a getaway and grabbed it before some ribbon cutting or benefit dinner got in her way." Carrie laughed.

"And you? Doing the same as your mother?"

A shaky laugh escaped her. "This is sounding suspiciously like an interview."

"Not at all. Just me getting to know you."

She raised a suspicious brow. "Really? Why?"

"Because it's not every day that a man meets a princess. A beautiful princess, at that."

"Flattery." She waved off the words.

"Truth. If this was really an interview, I'd take notes or have a recorder. I don't have either." He put out his hands to prove the point. "Though, if you ever reconsider, it would be really interesting for the public to get to know an unconventional princess."

She laughed. "Unconventional? Me?"

"You seem like one to me. So unconventional, it's

almost hard to believe you're royalty." He watched her face for a reaction to the accusation, but Carrie's remained pensive.

"Unconventional," she repeated. "I like that."

She said the words softly, drawing him in, making him feel bad for swinging the conversation around to what he ultimately wanted from her. He reminded himself that he was a journalist, and a journalist always puts the story first. Hadn't his father drummed that into him?

"And that's the side of you I want to portray in an interview," he said. "Don't you think the world should get to know the real you?"

"The real me." She considered his words for a long moment, then flashed another one of those million-dollar smiles his way. "Okay. Let's do the interview."

"Great." He'd just landed his first piece for *Inside Scoop.* Maybe now he could finally begin to relax and feel like life here in Indiana was going to work out for him and Annabelle. Still, a vague sense of unease, as if he'd left something undone, or more, he was taking a wrong turn, plagued him. It was just this past year, he'd decided, catching up with him. He needed to focus on his job. "I promise, it'll be okay, and it won't be some fluff piece. We can set it up for—"

She put up a hand. "I have one condition."

"A condition?" Here it came. No questions about her as the princess. No focus on her connection to the royal family—or lack thereof. That would do him no good. He'd get more mileage out of the story of the dog nursing a litter of kittens.

"I want to focus on the real reason I'm here in America," Carrie said. "And nothing else."

* * *

She'd left him at a loss for words. Not for long, Carrie was sure. Well, good. She'd wanted to turn the tables on the reporter, and turn this situation to her advantage. She wasn't wild at all about the idea of being interviewed—the media had always seemed like more of a curse than a help—but if she was going to do this, then she wanted to retain control.

That meant no more fluff pieces on the life of a royal. She'd use this interview to increase the popularity of Uccelli's wines and in the process, build her case for taking over the vineyard's marketing and sales department. And Daniel Reynolds was the key to that plan.

Annabelle dashed over, interrupting Carrie's thoughts. Her hair had fallen out of its crown and was flying about her face in a wild halo, the tiara tangled and dangling on one side. "Let me fix that," Daniel said as he reached for her.

Annabelle jerked back. "No, Daddy. I don't want you to."

He pulled a comb from his back pocket. "I don't want your hair getting caught on the swings. Let me—"

"No, Daddy." She shied back, pressing a palm to her unruly curls. "It ouches when you brush my hair. I want Grandma to do it. She doesn't ouch."

A look of helplessness and regret came over Daniel's face, and Carrie saw him struggle to find something to say. Last night at the library, and today, she had seen the walls between father and daughter. There was a disconnect here, one that she could relate to. Too well.

How often had she tried to get through to her father, to make him understand that his youngest child wanted something else for her life? That she wasn't interested in the royal life that fascinated him so? Or in any of the career dreams he'd had for her? Her father had become more open to his daughter's input since Mariabella had blazed the trail a year ago, but still, there were times when Franco Santaro held tight to his Old World traditions and patriarchal opinions. And that ouched, as Annabelle would say.

"Girl hair is awful complicated, huh?" Carrie said to Annabelle.

Annabelle nodded.

"Want me to do it for you?"

Annabelle shot her father a wary glance, but he was already handing the comb to Carrie, clearly glad to abdicate that responsibility. Annabelle plopped onto the blanket before Carrie, and sat still while Carrie gently tugged the tiara out and then started to comb. "I know lots about hair," she said. "I have two sisters. Every day, each of us wanted a different hairstyle."

"Did your daddy do your hair, too?"

Carrie laughed at the thought of her big, gruff father, the king, handling a hairbrush. She smoothed the top of Annabelle's hair and nestled the tiara back in place. "No, he didn't. My mother did."

"Oh. My mommy died." Annabelle bit her lower lip and her eyes welled. "That's how's come Daddy has to do my hair."

Carrie's heart broke. Three words, and a peek inside a little girl's fragile world, upended in an instant by tragedy. Silence extended between the three of them. A shadow fell over Daniel's face.

Somehow, knowing he was a widower changed her perception about him. He had been married, experienced a tragic loss, and those things softened her image of him. Maybe he wasn't the evil reporter she'd thought.

She peered around the little girl's curls, taking in the sight of Annabelle's down-turned face. Carrie wanted to do something, anything, to take that sadness away. She handed the comb back to Daniel, who looked hurt and…well, lost.

Carrie leaned in closer to Annabelle. "Why don't I help you be the bestest princess ever, Annabelle?"

"Really?" Annabelle's nose crinkled, the somber mood lifted. "How?"

"Well…" And then Carrie realized she'd been as far from being a princess as one could possibly be, and thus, didn't have the tiara, ball gown, finding Prince Charming experience that a little girl like Annabelle would be looking for. "How about we start with simple things?"

Annabelle popped up onto her knees, her blue eyes no longer clouded by grief, but bright and animated. "Like what?"

"Like the princess walk." Carrie got to her feet and put out a hand to Annabelle. She took a step forward, giving her hips a slight saunter as she did. "You swish-swish as you walk."

"Swish-swish?"

"Watch my dress." Carrie took several steps forward, exaggerating her steps so her sundress would swing around her ankles. "If you're very, very quiet, you can hear the dress going *swish-swish.* When my sisters and I were little, we did this all the time." The three Santaro girls had princess-walked all through the castle, their giggles bouncing off the tall stone walls. Their etiquette coach had watched with stern disapproval, while all her hard work at creating proper, demure young ladies was undone.

Annabelle followed in Carrie's footsteps. The tulle beneath her dress whispered with each movement. Annabelle giggled. "I swish-swished. Am I a princess now?"

Carrie pressed a finger to Annabelle's button nose. "I think you are. But you have to practice walking a lot."

"Okay." She whirled back to the picnic, grabbed her stuffed dog and held the toy in front of her. "Come on, Whitney. I'm gonna show you how to walk like a princess." Then she dashed down the hill, the dog tucked tight under her arm.

Carrie returned to the blanket and sat down beside Daniel. "She's so cute."

He flashed her a grateful smile. "Thank you. You made her day."

"It was nothing."

"It was more than that," he said. A hint of vulnerability edged his words. "She needs a strong female presence in her life. She has her grandmother, but..." He shook his head, then sighed. "It's been hard since her mother died."

"I'm sorry." She watched Annabelle dart across the grassy park. How tragic that such a young girl would lose her mother. "If you don't mind my asking, what happened?"

For a long moment, Daniel remained silent. Carrie wished she could take the question back. Then he began to speak. "It was a car accident," he said, his voice low and soft, filled with a pain Carrie couldn't even begin to understand. "She was supposed to work late that night, but then I got called out of town on an assignment, so Sarah had to rush home to watch Annabelle so I could leave. It was raining, she was going too fast, and—" He shook his head.

"I'm so sorry, Daniel." Carrie reached out, laid a light touch on Daniel's arm. It didn't feel like enough, not nearly enough, to make up for such a loss.

"It's been a year, but sometimes it seems like yesterday." His gaze followed his daughter as she put her stuffed animal in one of the baby swings and began to push him back and forth. "Things between my late wife and I were...not good before she died, and we were about to divorce." He sighed, his gaze still on his daughter. "I just never imagined this was how I'd end up becoming a single father."

She couldn't imagine the struggles he faced. It made the pressures of her life seem petty in comparison. Her attitude toward him softened. "I'm sorry. I'm sure it's terribly hard."

He let out a short laugh, the sound bittersweet. "That's an understatement. I don't know anything about braids or tights or tea parties. I believe Annabelle has banned me from all future tea parties for not following the rules."

"My father was never good at them, either, so you're not the only one. Not that he had a lot of time to see us girls."

"Too busy running a country and all that?"

"Exactly." She crumpled up her empty paper plate, rose and tossed it into a nearby trash can. Then she retook her seat on the blanket, leaning back on her elbows to soak up a little of the warm summer sun. "I saw the nannies and maids more than I saw my parents when I was a little girl."

"I can relate."

A few short words, throwing up a verbal "don't ask" fence. Carrie knew she should let it go. And didn't. "Did your parents work a lot?"

"My father did. He defined the word *workaholic*."

"What did he do?"

"Wrote stories that changed the world." A hint of sarcasm tinged the sentence. "Those are his words, not mine. He was a Pulitzer-winning journalist. The kind who covered the stories no one else wanted to because they were too dangerous or too controversial."

"And did he?"

"Did he what?"

"Change the world?"

"In more ways than one." He let out a long breath. "I didn't come here to talk about me or my childhood."

"Then what did you come here for?"

"To get to know you better." Daniel stretched out on the blanket, opened the container of grapes and offered them to Carrie before taking a few in his palm.

Get to know her better. Solely for professional reasons? Or ones more personal?

She popped one in her mouth, then leaned back on her elbows, enjoying the warm kiss of the sun on her face, and the sweet-tart juice of the grapes. Instead of worrying about answers she didn't have.

"Thank you," he said.

"For what?"

"For making Annabelle smile. She doesn't do that often lately." Now he turned his own smile on her, and it hit her squarely in the gut.

Damn, the man was handsome. And the way he smiled—

Well, it made her forget almost everything she kept telling herself to remember. Faith's advice about having a fling came back to Carrie's mind. If she was going to have a fling during her time in Winter Haven, he'd be exactly the kind of man she'd choose.

Then she shook her head and tried to get back on track. He was a reporter. Not to be trusted. But the reasons why seemed very, very faraway.

"She's a wonderful little girl." Carrie watched Annabelle talking to her stuffed animal, her face alive, animated. "She reminds me of myself when I was that age."

"How so?"

"I was always off by myself, in my own world. And always getting in trouble for it, too." Carrie laughed.

He dropped a few more grapes into her palm, and a whisper of disappointment ran through her that he hadn't fed them to her, one at a time. Whoa, what was with her? She knew better than to get involved with a man like him—a reporter at that. But there was something about Daniel Reynolds, something vulnerable that peeked out every once in a while from his tough exterior. It made her wonder what else she'd learn if she got closer to him.

Much closer.

"I can see that about you," he said. "You strike me as the rebel type."

"Which isn't exactly princess material."

"But wouldn't that create more media coverage of you, rather than less?" He put out his hands. "I'm just doing my research. And I have to say, on the web, you're almost nonexistent."

"And the pictures you did find are all of me dressed at some event, right?"

He nodded. "They don't even look like you."

She let out a gust. "Because that isn't me. Not the

real me." Then she sighed. "There are two reasons why you won't find much information on me. For one, I tried to stay away from palace events as much as possible. I was always happier outside, working in the stables, the gardens, the vineyards. Anywhere that was open and free from castle life. I started working in the vineyard when I was eight. My father has always hated me spending time in the vineyard. He thinks I should have a career that's more…"

"Sedate?" Daniel supplied.

She laughed. "Yes. And more befitting a royal."

"And plucking grapes from a vine isn't?"

"Not at all. The last thing he wanted was pictures of me, up to my elbows in grape juice, splashed across the papers. My sister the art dealer made for great press. My middle sister, who had a career as a clothing designer before she became queen, was the kind who always grabbed the media eye."

"And your mother?" he said. "She vacationed in Winter Haven once."

Carrie nodded. "She did. Under an assumed name, so no one would know it was her. She spent a summer here, just living as an ordinary person. She said she chose Winter Haven because nothing is more ordinary and unroyal than the Midwest." Her gaze skipped across the park, past the dozens of families sharing moments of fun. Had her mother enjoyed these same moments? Or had there been more to attract her to Winter Haven? Of late, Bianca hadn't wanted to talk about the town, or her experiences here. "She loved it here. And…so do I."

"I don't think the newspapers ever knew your mother was here. I did a little research and couldn't find anything other than a couple of gossip columns.

But with you being more public about being here, I'm surprised the reporters haven't descended like flies."

She shrugged. "I'm not the heir. I'm not even the spare. I'm the third daughter, the extra, as the newspapers dubbed me the day I was born. Sort of like one too many cars in the garage."

He shook his head. "I can't believe anyone would ever say that about you."

"They said that. And a lot of other things. A long time ago, those words hurt. The media knows just where to stab for maximum blood." She exhaled. "I don't mean to include you in that group."

"I'm not like that. I didn't become a reporter to hurt people."

That allayed her fears. "I'm glad to hear that."

"Trust me now?"

"A little."

He grinned. "We're making progress. That's good."

"Yeah, it is." But progress toward what? she wondered.

"So why wine?" he asked.

"It wasn't where I started, that's for sure. It took me a lot of years and a lot of trial and error to find the job that truly fulfilled me. The one that was right for me. And it wasn't one that fit the royal image." She rolled the grapes around in her hand and watched the light green orbs bounce off each other. "When we harvest the grapes, we want every single one to be perfect. To be perfectly ripe, perfectly juicy and perfectly shaped. But there's always a few—some that are too small and never really grew, some that are too big and dwarfed the others, blocking their sun, and some entire vines that aren't as sweet this year as last. But really, in the end, it's the imperfect ones that make the best wine."

"How's that?"

"They lend a different flavor to the mix than the perfect ones do. When you blend the two together, you get a depth of flavor that you wouldn't if every single grape was the same. And it takes a mix of both to make our wines."

"Just as it takes a mix of personalities to make a royal family?"

She laughed. "Yes. At least that's what I think."

"I think it takes a mix to make any family."

She swallowed, then let her gaze connect with his. Damn, his eyes were the most vibrant shade of blue. She was falling for him, and falling fast. She needed to rein herself in, but for some reason, she couldn't find the willpower. "And what part of the mix are you?"

They were delving into personal territory, crossing over boundaries. And Carrie, who knew better, couldn't seem to put the brakes on the conversation. She wanted to know more about Daniel Reynolds, have another peek inside this man who, like her, didn't seem to fit his career moniker.

"Me?" Daniel said. "I'm the distant father. In one very bad way, I took after my father. I turned into the workaholic who missed so many moments that can't be done over. I thought I was providing for my family, continuing the Daniels' legacy. But I was like those grapes that are so large, they can't see what they're doing to the ones below them." Then, as if he realized he had said too much, Daniel reached for his water, took a sip and let out half a laugh. "Anyway, that's enough analysis for today, Dr. Freud."

"Is that why you live here now? Instead of New York?"

He arched a brow. "How did you know that?"

"I know how to use the internet, too, Mr. Reynolds." She grinned, and he laughed in response. She'd seen a few articles about him and bookmarked a few others to read later.

"Touché, Miss Santaro." He let out a long breath, his gaze on his daughter playing on the swing set. "When I lived in New York, it was hard on Annabelle, especially after she lost her mother. I worked so many hours and traveled so much that she had more in common with the nanny than with me."

"I can relate," Carrie said, echoing his earlier words.

Regret softened Daniel's features. "That's why I moved back home. At least here she has my mother, who loves her to death and spoils her mercilessly."

"Everyone needs a grandmother like that."

He turned to her, and his face took on a more animated cast. She could see him transition from personal Daniel to work Daniel. "That's why this story is so important to me. I promise to be fair and do a well-researched, nonsensational piece on you. But I need this, Carrie. I need to turn my career around, and I'll be honest with you, a piece on a princess is the kind that can do that for me. That'll allow me to stay here in Indiana and keep Annabelle near her family." He turned to his side, propping himself up on one elbow, and looked up at her. When he did, she could imagine herself falling into his blue eyes, being swept away by a man who was all wrong for her. He lived in America for one, he was a single father for another, and biggest strike of all—

He was a reporter. Whenever she was tempted to fall for him, she needed to remember that his number one goal was the story.

Not a relationship. And not one with her.

He'd just made that clear. He needed her story, so he could serve his own goals. God, why was she such a fool?

"So…what is the real reason you're here in America?" he asked. "You never told me."

She bit back a sigh and reminded herself that this was what she wanted, too—and in the end, she'd be happier with a vineyard than with a man. Then why did disappointment sting so bad?

"A year ago, I started working in the import/export division of the Uccelli Vineyards, helping with sales and marketing. I've worked in all the other parts, from planting to harvesting to bottling. The more I worked there, the more I wanted to learn. Then I realized the key to helping the company grow was to bring Uccelli wines to the American market. When an opportunity to work in the first shop carrying our wines arose, I took it."

"All part of learning the business inside and out?"

She nodded, then reached for her water and took a sip. "Yes."

He considered her answer for a moment. Across the park, Annabelle was dancing around the swing set with Whitney as her waltz partner. Daniel's features softened, and a smile curved across his face.

"Have you ever been married?" he asked without turning to look at her.

The change in conversational direction took her back. Was he trying to keep her off-kilter or had she been wrong, and he really was intrigued on a personal level? "Me? No. I've never even come close."

"I find that hard to believe. A beautiful woman like you."

"Well, it's true. Princesses aren't as high in demand as you'd think."

"Well, around here, princesses aren't as common as you'd think."

She laughed. "True."

"The other princesses in your family are married."

She sipped at her water, watching him, trying to assess his motives. "Actually, only Mariabella is married. Allegra, who became queen after my parents stepped down, hasn't married yet. She's engaged, and if we can ever pin her down to a date, she'll get married, too." Then she put the water bottle aside and crossed her arms over her chest. "Why the sudden interest in my marital status? Is this an interview?"

"It's…" An uncomfortable look came over his face, but she refused to look away. "Well, it's research."

The words hit her like ice. She should have known better. Should have listened to her instincts. That's what happened when she got too far from the castle. She relaxed, let down her guard and believed she could be just like any other woman. "I thought you invited me on this picnic because you were interested in me. *Me,* not my status as a member of the royal family." She let out a gust. "So is this it? Your whole plan? Do you have a microphone stashed somewhere I don't know about?"

"No, no microphones. I swear. When we do the interview, it'll be in the studio."

Something flickered in his eyes. "What aren't you telling me?"

He exhaled a long breath. "My boss has this idea. Based on *The Princess and the Pea* book. He wants to…"

"Wants to what?" Even as she asked the question, she knew the answer.

"Do a princess test." Daniel put up his hands. "I had nothing to do with it. Apparently, my boss thought it would be a good idea to do a *Princess and the Pea* type approach to the story. I tried to argue against it, but he insisted. And he, unfortunately, is the boss."

She laughed, but the sound was hollow. "How on earth are you going to conduct such a test? Are you going to have me lie on twenty mattresses?"

"I honestly don't know." Daniel let out a breath. "I'm sorry, Carrie. If there was anything I could have done—"

She jerked to her feet and grabbed her tote bag. The wine bottle bumped against her waist. Carrie yanked the bottle out and dropped it onto the soft blanket. The pinot landed with a thud, the golden liquid inside glistening in the sun. "I don't need to take a test to prove who I am. You want to know who Carlita Santaro is? Look in there. Everything you want to know about me is in that bottle. That's where my heart is. That's where my soul is. Not in a stone castle. And not in some ridiculous test."

Then she turned on her heel and left before she spent one more second believing her attraction to this man was anything other than a fairy tale.

CHAPTER FIVE

DANIEL packed up the picnic, folded up the blanket and then faced one very disappointed little girl. "She said she had to leave early. I'm sorry."

Annabelle pouted and glared at her father. He was clearly not on her favorite people list today. "But I had a present for her. And you said I could give her my present."

"I know I did, honey, but—"

"Daddy! You promised!" She stomped her foot on the blanket, sending one of the water bottles skittering across the grass.

"Belle, you need to behave. This is no way to—"

"And you're s'posed to keep your promises." Her anger melted, replaced by a sadness that seemed to fill her eyes until they became wide cornflower-blue saucers. "You told me you would."

The last was added in a whisper, but Daniel felt the words like a knife to his heart. A year ago, he'd sat down with Belle on her little twin bed, and held her while she cried. She'd wanted some assurance that her world would turn right-side-up again, and he'd wanted only to give that to her. So he'd told her that from that day forward, he would keep every promise he made her.

At first, he'd broken little ones—*I promise I'll be*

home in time for dinner, he'd say in the morning, and then he'd get home a half hour after the last pan had been washed by the nanny. Then bigger things—*I promise I'll be there for your first day of preschool,* forgetting that would be the day the president would be visiting New York, pulling Daniel away for a long day and even longer night. By the time he realized he'd broken the most fundamental promise of all—*I promise I'll be there to tuck you in every night*—the look of mistrust and disappointment had become a constant shadow in Annabelle's eyes.

So he'd come to Winter Haven, vowing to do better, to be better. And here he was, falling into the same pattern all over again.

Becoming his father.

How was he ever going to win the war between being a good father and being a good journalist? Maybe he was asking too much. Maybe it was impossible.

He bent down to Annabelle's level. Her pixie face was filled with stern judgment, but her lips trembled and her eyes shone with unshed tears. Damn. Every time he turned around, he made things worse. "I did promise you, didn't I?"

She nodded.

He let out a breath. Who knew this parenting thing would be so hard? That one man could make so many mistakes? He might not be able to rectify the ones in the past, but he could fix this one. "Well then, let's finish packing up and go."

"Go home? But Daddy—"

"No, not home." He took Annabelle's delicate hand in his own. She was so trusting, and so many times in the past year he had screwed that up. Well, no more. "We're going to see the princess."

As the words sank in, a burst of happy sunshine glowed in Annabelle's features. "Really?"

He nodded, then hoisted the blanket and cooler into his arm. "Yep. Because you have a gift for her. And I have something for her, too."

"You got a gift, too, Daddy?"

"No. I have something else." He started up the hill, Annabelle in tow. "An apology."

Carrie had reread the same page three times. Her eyes skimmed over the scene before her, but the words refused to assemble in her brain into any form of a story. It wasn't that the novel was dull—it was her mind.

She couldn't focus. Her attention drifted between the library book in her hands and the view outside the cozy window seat, but her mind was really on Daniel Reynolds.

Why did she keep thinking about him? He wanted only one thing from her—an interview that would boost his career. Not that she could blame him. After all, wasn't she looking for the same thing?

Except…she'd gone on the picnic today intending to use him to achieve her own goals, then found herself getting wrapped up in him, in Annabelle, but most of all, in his eyes. His smile. His voice. How sexy he'd looked, stretched out on the plaid blanket, popping grapes into his mouth as they talked.

And she'd started wondering if living this rather ordinary life in a country far from home could come with a rather ordinary romance, the kind millions of women had every year, but Carrie had never enjoyed. She'd seen the media firestorm that followed her sisters on every date they took—paparazzi camped outside restaurants, perched in trees at church. They watched and photographed Mariabella's and Allegra's every move, speculated about every kiss, every smile. Once Mariabella married last year, the frenzy had shifted to Allegra, and become a nuclear explosion of interest once she ascended to the crown.

Carrie, as the third daughter and the furthest from the throne, was often, thankfully, forgotten by the media. Her two older, more glamorous and more social sisters captured the spotlight while Carrie was more than happy to stay out of the glare. But still, Carrie had had her share of reporters trying to spy on her dates. Enough that she'd avoided dating as much as possible. What would it be like to be here, in the middle of nowhere, and go out on a date without worries about the next day's headlines?

The doorbell rang, jarring Carrie out of her thoughts. She set her book on the bench, then crossed to the front door. Few people knew she was staying here, so who would be coming by on a Sunday night?

Through the oval glass, she saw a familiar tiara and laughed to herself. Annabelle Reynolds, still wearing her princess clothes. Then Carrie drew up short. Annabelle would undoubtedly be accompanied by her father.

"What are you doing here?" Carrie said when she opened the door. She kept her tone neutral, the kind of regal dismissive voice that she pulled out every once in a while. It was the voice that said stay away, that put distance between herself and people who tried to get close. But Daniel Reynolds must not have heard the imperious tone, because he took a step closer and offered up a lopsided grin. "And how did you find out where I was staying?"

"Wasn't hard. There aren't many princesses renting cottages in Winter Haven."

"Oh." Her face heated. She hadn't thought of the news her rental would create around town.

"I'm sorry for coming by your house," Daniel said, "but Annabelle wanted to give you something today and you left the picnic so quickly, she didn't get a chance. And I wanted to say I was sorry."

Guilt ran through Carrie. Here she'd been thinking the worst about Daniel Reynolds's motives and he'd been here merely to apologize and keep a promise to his little girl. She bent down to Annabelle's level. "You have something for me?"

Annabelle nodded, and the tiara teetered in her golden curls. "Uh-huh. A present."

"A present? Well, now I'm curious." She smiled. "But I think such a special event calls for a few cookies first."

"I love cookies!"

"Good. Come on in, then." Carrie stepped back and waved them into the house.

Annabelle dashed forward and spun a circle in the small living room of the lake cottage, taking in the cozy furnishings and multiple windows that formed the basis of the small house. "This is so pretty. It's like...where Snow White lived."

Carrie laughed. "It is, isn't it?"

Daniel leaned in toward her. "Any dwarves lingering about?"

"Sorry, no. Today is their day off."

He chuckled. "And here I thought I'd find servants underfoot and a butler at the door."

"Goodness, no. It's nice to be alone. And I don't even mind doing the dishes or cleaning the bathrooms."

She realized as she said the words, they were true. She'd spent so many years having others do for her even the simplest of life's needs that to do them herself had been a nice burst of freedom. "Though I'm probably not very good at it."

"Did you bake the cookies, too?" he said as he followed her into the kitchen.

"My domestic skills don't extend to the stove. Though I can whip up a mean batch of scrambled eggs if the occasion arises. But that's it. Don't expect a gourmet meal from these hands."

"I can't cook at all, either." He tossed her a grin, and something warm filled his blue eyes. "We'd be no good together. We'd probably starve."

The words implied a future. A relationship. Even as she knew she shouldn't imagine it, the sentence sent a little thrill through Carrie. For a second, she pictured them standing in the kitchen, debating over take-out options, then ending the discussion with a compromise…and a kiss. "We'd, uh, have to order in," she said. "Often."

His gaze darkened and a smile slowly curved across his face. "Yeah, we would."

"And maybe we'd fight over Chinese versus pizza." She had moved closer to him, ostensibly to reach for a coffee mug, but her hand didn't connect with anything.

"We wouldn't fight." The smile turned into a grin and he took a half step closer. Heat filled the space between them, and the air seemed to still. Far in the distance, a motorboat revved, its engine going from low to high. "Because a smart man lets the woman have whatever she wants."

Carrie's breath caught. It was as if she had run ten miles and suddenly stopped. Her heart raced, her lungs sought air. And all she could see were Daniel's blue eyes. "And why is that?"

"Because a happy woman makes a happy home. And that makes for a very, very happy man."

He had moved even closer and Carrie's thoughts tumbled like rocks down a hill. Would he kiss her? Did she want him to? Her pulse thundered in her ears. How long had it been since she'd been kissed—really, truly kissed?

Too long. *Way* too long.

Carrie opened her mouth, began to push the question past her lips. "Daniel—"

"Daddy! I got to give Princess Carrie her present."

Annabelle's voice made them jerk apart. Daniel spun toward his daughter. "Oh, yeah. The, uh, present. That's right, pumpkin. I forgot again. Sorry."

Annabelle thrust a bright pink bag in Carrie's direction. "Here. For you."

"Thank you." Carrie took the bag and held it to her chest. A part of her sent up a silent thank-you for Annabelle's interruption. Carrie had nearly made a crazy, impulsive decision that would have had huge ramifications. How many times had she done that? Acted first, and thought later? She turned her attention to Annabelle...the smartest choice right now. "But first, I believe I promised you some cookies."

"Yes..." She glanced at her father. "Please."

Carrie grabbed a plastic container on the counter, peeled off the lid and held it out to Annabelle. An assortment of cookies—all courtesy of the Winter Haven grocery store—filled the box. "Pick as many as you like."

"Uh, pick two," Daniel said, waving a hand in front

of Annabelle's eager reach. "We haven't had dinner yet."

"I want this one and..." Annabelle pulled out a double chocolate, then wavered between one with sprinkles and one with frosting. She glanced up at her father. "Daddy, can I have three? *Please?*"

Daniel remained firm for another few seconds, then his stern look faded into one of indulgence and Carrie's resistance to him ebbed even more. "Okay, but you're going to have to eat all your dinner later."

"I will! I promise!" Annabelle snatched up both the sprinkled and frosted cookies, then scrambled into a kitchen chair. Crumbs scattered across the maple surface of the table.

Carrie poured her a glass of milk, then got both Daniel and herself a cup of coffee. The two of them joined Annabelle—who had already eaten most of her first cookie. Carrie laid the satiny pink bag on the table. "Shall I open this now?"

Annabelle nodded. "Uh-huh."

Carrie reached for the drawstring, then stopped. "Hmm...I wonder what's in here?"

Daniel put up his hands. "I had nothing to do with it, so if it's a monkey, it's not my fault."

"Daddy! It's not a monkey." Annabelle rolled her eyes in exasperation. "You won't let me have one."

"For very good reasons." A tease lit Daniel's eyes.

"Monkeys are fun. And funny." Annabelle propped her chin on her hands. "I want one."

"I don't think you do. They can be terrible pets," Carrie said. "We had one in the castle for a little while."

"You did?" Annabelle's eyes widened. "Was he yours?"

"He was a gift from the president of South Africa.

One of my sisters mentioned wanting a monkey when he was visiting, and lo and behold, a live monkey was on our doorstep a week later."

"What did you do?" Daniel asked.

"My father took one look at it and called the zoo. Allegra was so angry, she didn't talk to him for a whole week. She visited that monkey at the zoo constantly for a full year." Carrie reached for the drawstring on the bag. "I'm dying to see what's in here. Hmm…what present did Miss Annabelle bring me?"

That was enough to redirect Annabelle's attention away from monkeys. Daniel mouthed a silent thank-you over his daughter's head, and the moment of détente sent a whisper of desire running through Carrie. It was all so ordinary, so sweet, so…domestic.

Could this be her life someday? Sitting at the kitchen table with her husband and her child, sharing laughs and smiles?

But then Carrie opened the bag and pulled out a slim plastic rhinestone-studded headband and was reminded of who she was and where she belonged. "Why, it's a tiara. And it's beautiful."

"I got two," Annabelle said. "So I gave you that one, 'cuz you forgot yours in Yousilly."

Carrie bit back a laugh at Belle's version of Uccelli. "I did indeed."

Annabelle pointed to the tiara in Carrie's hand, then at her own, and grinned. "Now we can be princesses together."

How could Carrie resist such a sweet idea? She settled the rhinestone headband on top of her head, pushing down gently until the comb corners caught and held. "How do I look?"

Annabelle giggled. "Like a princess."

"So do you." Carrie swiped a finger across Annabelle's button nose. "You're the prettiest princess I've ever seen, Annabelle."

Sunshine filled Annabelle's features, and she scrambled out of the chair to spin a quick twirl in the kitchen, sending her frothy dress spiraling outward like a bell. Then she started moving faster and faster, whirling until she was nearly a blur. "I'm a princess!"

"Okay, okay," Daniel said, putting a hand on his daughter's arm to slow her spin. "I think someone's had enough cookies."

Annabelle came to a reluctant stop. "One more? Please?"

"Nope," Daniel said. "You have to leave room for dinner or Grandma will be sad."

Carrie pushed the cookie container to the side so it wouldn't tempt a certain little girl. "Would you like to watch a movie instead? Or some cartoons?"

Annabelle nodded, and followed Carrie out of the kitchen and into the living room. She settled on the sofa, and within seconds after Carrie had flipped on the television, Annabelle was falling asleep. The plastic headband rose up and down on her head with each soft breath.

"You should take that off her," Carrie said to Daniel.

"Take what off?"

"The crown. Not even real princesses sleep in their crown." She tossed him a smile.

He sighed, then took a step forward and slid the rhinestone piece out of Annabelle's hair, and left it on the coffee table. His gaze lingered on the tiara for a long moment. "I'm always forgetting the little things."

They headed back into the kitchen, returning to the table and their coffee. The TV played softly in the background, orchestral music underscoring the antics of a frustrated cat and a wily mouse.

Daniel ran a hand through his hair, displacing the dark waves. The slight bit of messiness only added to his appeal and gave his features a sexier edge. Carrie chided herself mentally for thinking about kissing Daniel Reynolds when they were talking about his parenting.

Except kissing him was the only thing she'd been thinking about since that moment in her kitchen earlier. Heck, since she'd met him.

She'd dated men—not a lot because there weren't many guys who wanted the pressure of a royal girlfriend—but like with her career choices, she'd never stuck to any one. The men she'd met had either been too dull or too wowed by her royal status.

Daniel was neither. He was…ordinary, but in an extraordinary way. And that was appealing. Very appealing.

"The funny thing is, I was great at my job," Daniel said, drawing her back to the conversation. "There was no challenge that I didn't take on, no assignment I turned down. Without a second thought, I'd fly to a war zone and report on the latest battle, helicopter in to a national disaster and spend three days living out of a duffel bag and a tent. But raising my daughter alone—" he shook his head, and his gaze strayed to the tuft of blond curls peeking over the arm of the sofa "—that's the scariest damned thing I've ever done. I'm always afraid I'm going to screw it up."

"Oh, I don't think you will. You love her, and that covers a lot of ground."

"Does it?" Vulnerability shimmered in his eyes and Carrie wanted to promise him everything would be wonderful from this moment forward, that they would all get their fairy-tale ending. But she couldn't. Even a princess couldn't promise happily ever after.

"Obviously you're doing something right," Carrie said. "Annabelle seems like a wonderful girl."

"She is. I'm blessed that way. But when I think about the days ahead—those teenage years, the first date, the prom, heck, her wedding—I realize that I am so beyond underequipped for this job." He wrapped his hands around the white ceramic mug and gave it a spin back and forth. "A few months ago, she asked me to braid her hair. I forget why, something to do with being Rapunzel for the day or something. I spent twenty frustrating minutes trying to figure out how to do it, before I finally had to look up directions on the internet. What kind of father can't do something as simple as that?"

Carrie reached across the table and laid her hand on top of his. Warmth met her palm. He lifted his gaze to hers, and her heart melted. "One who is trying his best."

"I don't know about that."

"I'm no expert," she said, "but I think you're doing just fine."

A smile curved across his face. "Thank you."

In that instant, the simple touch Carrie had started took on new meaning and dimension. Every nerve in her body attuned to the feel of her hand on top of his larger, stronger one. She could feel the ridge of his knuckles, the pulse of his veins, the taut skin that covered his hand. She wanted him, in ways that had nothing to do with a simple friendly touch. Dangerous ground to tread.

She jerked away and got to her feet. "Uh, do you want, uh, a refill?"

Never in her life had she felt this discombobulated. This…out of sorts. Like all control had suddenly slipped away, and a part of her that had never spoken before was taking charge. She grabbed his mug without waiting for an answer and turned to the counter. Her hand shook as she poured and the coffee spilled onto the counter in a wide brown arc.

"You're going to burn yourself." Daniel's voice, behind her.

She stilled. Her heart hammered in her chest. She tried to remind herself that he was a reporter. That he had an ulterior motive for being with her. But her mind kept dancing away from the truth and flirting instead with the idea of kissing him. Of being held by him. Of taking him down the hall to the little blue-and-white bedroom and exploring every inch of Daniel Reynolds.

"Sorry. I…I made a mess." She reached for a sponge, but Daniel laid a hand on her arm. His touch sent electricity running through her veins. Her heart skipped a beat, her pulse skittered, and she had to remind herself to breathe.

"I don't want any more coffee, Carrie."

"Oh, uh, okay."

He tugged on her arm until she turned to face him. "I don't want any more coffee," he repeated, his voice lower and darker now.

The TV played a soft undertow in the next room. Outside on the water, the motorboat sped around the lake, a constant quiet roar. But inside the small twelve-by-fifteen kitchen, another kind of roar was growing inside Carrie. She swallowed, then expelled the bigger question in one long breath. "What do you want, Daniel?"

"This." He reached up, cupped her jaw with his hands in a move so tender and gentle, it nearly made her cry. Then he leaned in, inch by torturous inch, and whispered his lips across hers.

It was a taste, nothing more. A quick brush of his mouth against hers, short enough to give her a chance to change her mind. If Carrie was smart, she'd push him away. Stop this now, before it got out of control.

She didn't move.

Didn't breathe.

Didn't say a word.

"And I want this," he whispered, and leaned in even farther until his mouth fully joined with hers and their kiss became a dance of discovery and desire. Heat exploded inside her, and her body buzzed with desire. In an instant, she went from zero to sixty with want.

"Daniel," she whispered, then opened against him, her hands sliding up his back to clutch at his shoulders, to pull him even closer. No distance separated their bodies now, and every inch of Carrie tingled. But still, she wanted more, wanted…everything. Now, right now.

His tongue slid against hers, a sexy little move that sent a shiver down her spine. She answered with a darting caress of her own and he groaned. His fingers tangled in her hair and liquid heat pooled deep inside her. Their kiss deepened, turned from tasting to ravishing, and Carrie had a split second to think how this was what she had been looking for all her life.

When Daniel finally pulled back, his breath still coming fast and dark desire still lingering in his eyes,

Carrie swore she heard a sigh of disappointment. From him? Or from her?

"That, uh, definitely isn't coffee," she said.

He laughed. "No, it isn't."

"Was it a mistake?"

He danced his fingers along her jaw. His blue eyes looked like the ocean on a stormy day. She felt as if she could stare into those eyes forever and never fully plumb their depths. "I don't know," he said. "It's been a long time since I've dated anyone."

"Me, too."

"And I've never dated anyone I was interviewing."

"I've never dated a reporter."

"Then should we stop now?"

She looked at his handsome face, the defined jawline, the deep stormy eyes set beneath a shock of dark hair. All she wanted to do was touch him, learn him, know him. She stepped back into his arms and tilted her chin to meet his. "Maybe later. Much later."

He grinned, then drew her to him and kissed her again.

CHAPTER SIX

THEY came up for air a long while later. The kiss still burned in Daniel's mind, and he wanted nothing more than to go back to kissing Carrie. But first, work.

"As nice as that was," he said, grinning, "I didn't come here for that."

"No?"

"Well, maybe." The grin widened. Then he sobered. "I really came to apologize. I shouldn't have sprung the princess test on you. I don't want to be that kind of reporter. I wanted to prove or disprove your identity, of course, but not in some crazy circus of a test."

"And did you?"

"Did I what?"

"Prove who I am?"

His gaze met hers, and in those wide brown eyes, he saw the answers he'd been seeking all day. He'd learned a long time ago to trust his gut when it came to a story, and right now, his gut was saying only one thing. "Yes, princess."

She smiled at him, and a switch flipped inside of Daniel. "So what now?"

"I was thinking—" he reached for her hand, needing to touch her, even as he knew he should try to keep this business-only "—maybe we could work together on developing this test thing. My boss is really stuck on the idea, but if we control it instead of him—"

"We'll end up with something that pleases everyone." She considered that for a moment, her fingers drifting against his palm. Every touch made it harder for him to concentrate. "And maybe if we kept it fun and light, it wouldn't be…"

"Humiliating."

"Exactly."

He lifted his hand and hers. "So we have a deal?"

"We do."

He shook hands with her, then raised her hand to his lips and sealed the deal with a kiss. "Good."

He heard Annabelle stirring in the next room. He glanced at the clock and realized it was nearly dinnertime. "I hate to say this, but I have to go soon. My mother has something cooking for dinner…" He grinned at her again. "Why don't you come, too?"

"I couldn't possibly. She's not expecting me and—"

"My mother loves company. And I'm sure she's going to love you."

A little while later, they were in Daniel's car, heading across Winter Haven. Annabelle talked the entire way home. The short nap on Carrie's sofa had clearly recharged his daughter's batteries—and then some. Daniel hadn't heard her chatter that much in months and months, and the constant rhythm of her voice warmed his heart. Had she finally turned the corner on her grief?

Or did it have more to do with Carrie Santaro's easy way with Annabelle? He had to admit, Carrie had managed to get Annabelle to open up in ways no one else had in the past year. The first clue? Her running off to the playground by herself. Ever since Sarah died,

Annabelle had glued herself to Daniel's side whenever they were out in public, as if she was afraid he, too, would leave her. But today—

Today, she'd run off and played for a solid hour. Lost in the imaginative world of a child. Then, back at Carrie's house, she'd laughed, she'd talked, she'd danced. After Annabelle's nap, Carrie had set up a tea party in the kitchen and played along with Annabelle and Whitney for a half hour. Annabelle had been delighted that Carrie pretended with her, acting as if they were two princesses using their best manners to sip imaginary tea and nibble on invisible treats. Daniel had watched it all with a growing happiness that told him maybe, just maybe, his daughter and he would finally be okay.

He glanced over at her and the urge to kiss Carrie roared in his chest. Damn. He couldn't think of that woman without thinking of kissing her—and more. The kisses they'd shared in her kitchen had started out sweet and slow, then quickly progressed to hot and amazing. She'd been as engaged as him—her hands roaming his back, her body pressed to his, her mouth awakening parts of him he'd thought had died.

When Carrie had moaned and whispered his name against his mouth, Daniel nearly hauled her off to the bedroom. If Annabelle hadn't been in the next room—

Well, she had been, and it was probably a good thing, too. He was moving too fast, getting involved before he thought it through.

And he knew from experience what a mistake that could be. For the hundredth time, he reminded himself to focus on work. Not the beautiful, intriguing princess.

* * *

"I don't think I've ever seen anyone smile so much," Faith said as the last customer of the day left By the Glass on Monday evening. She flipped the sign to Closed, then shot Carrie a grin. "It's either your birthday or you met a man."

Carrie laughed. "Well…it's not my birthday."

"Ooh, a man! I need to hear this. Let's go grab some coffees at the shop on the corner and you can tell me all about him."

Carrie started to say no. Years of living in a household and at a boarding school where everything you said was heard by a dozen people and eventually leaked to the media for their newest headline had conditioned her to be cautious, to keep her personal life close to her chest. But she wasn't in Uccelli right now. She was in Winter Haven, Indiana, and she was a girl who'd met a cute guy and wanted to share the details with her new friend. "Sounds like a great idea. Let me just grab my purse."

A minute later, the two of them headed out of the shop. They walked the two blocks to the small coffee shop that fronted the corner of Washington and Elm as the sun finished setting, bathing the town in an inky purple light. The pungent notes of fresh brewed coffee and newly baked goodies wafted to greet them as they stepped inside and grabbed a table in the corner. Faith got them two iced lattes and a brownie to split. She laid the plate before them, handed Carrie a fork, then propped her chin in her hands. "Okay, tell me everything."

Before Carrie could speak, an older woman stopped at their table. Her stylish gray hair offset her cranberry top and chunky gold necklace. "Excuse me. Are you Princess Carlita?"

"Yes."

The woman smiled. "I thought so. You look just like your mother."

"Thank you. Did you know her?"

The woman nodded. "Back then, I owned a little grocery store on the corner of Main and Elm. I sold it to Ernie Waller back in '98, but when your mother was here, it was known as Irma's Stop and Shop. I'm Irma." She pressed a hand to her chest. "Your mother came in every week, like clockwork. She always bought tea and cookies."

Carrie laughed. "That's my mother. She still likes to have that for breakfast."

"She was a lovely woman. Charmed everyone she met here. And probably broke a few hearts when she left." Irma smiled. "Why, I think half the town was in love with her."

"I'm not surprised," Carrie said. "The people of our country think the world of my mother. She's really good with people."

"She definitely was. And I know for a fact, more than a few men in town thought so, too." Irma winked.

Something in Irma's tone raised a red flag in Carrie. She tried to brush it off and attribute the reference to typical small-town gossip but the doubts stayed in the back of her mind. The mental puzzle tried to fit, but didn't. A missing piece? Or was she merely grabbing at invisible straws?

"Well, I'll be sure to tell her I ran into you the next time I talk to her."

"I'd appreciate that," Irma said. "Your mother made a lot of friends while she was here. I always thought she'd be back."

"Maybe someday she will." Carrie smiled.

The Reader Service—Here's How It Works:

BUSINESS REPLY MAIL
FIRST-CLASS MAIL   PERMIT NO. 717   BUFFALO, NY

POSTAGE WILL BE PAID BY ADDRESSEE

THE READER SERVICE
PO BOX 1867
BUFFALO NY 14240-9952

If offer card is missing write to: The Reader Service, P.O. Box 1867, Buffalo NY 14240-1867 or visit www.ReaderService.com

NO POSTAGE
NECESSARY
IF MAILED
IN THE
UNITED STATES

R-R-H 60/11

GET FREE BOOKS and FREE GIFTS WHEN YOU PLAY THE...

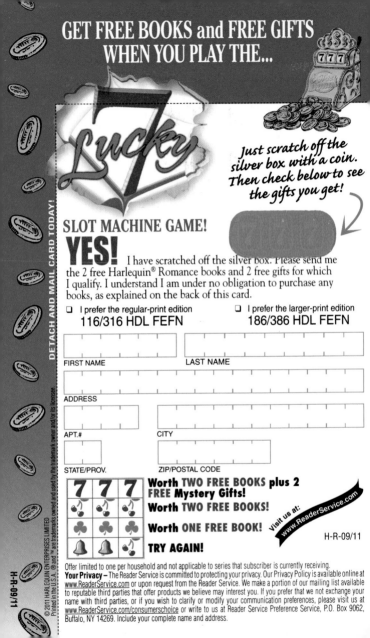

Lucky 7

Just scratch off the silver box with a coin. Then check below to see the gifts you get!

SLOT MACHINE GAME!

YES!

I have scratched off the silver box. Please send me the 2 free Harlequin® Romance books and 2 free gifts for which I qualify. I understand I am under no obligation to purchase any books, as explained on the back of this card.

☐ I prefer the regular-print edition
116/316 HDL FEFN

☐ I prefer the larger-print edition
186/386 HDL FEFN

FIRST NAME

LAST NAME

ADDRESS

APT.#

CITY

STATE/PROV.

ZIP/POSTAL CODE

7 7 7 Worth TWO FREE BOOKS plus 2 FREE Mystery Gifts!

🍒🍒🍒 Worth TWO FREE BOOKS!

♣♣♣ Worth ONE FREE BOOK!

🔔🔔🍒 TRY AGAIN!

Visit us at: www.ReaderService.com

H-R-09/11

DETACH AND MAIL CARD TODAY!

© 2011 HARLEQUIN ENTERPRISES LIMITED
Printed in the U.S.A. ® and ™ are trademarks owned and used by the trademark owner and/or its licensee.

Offer limited to one per household and not applicable to series that subscriber is currently receiving.
Your Privacy – The Reader Service is committed to protecting your privacy. Our Privacy Policy is available online at www.ReaderService.com or upon request from the Reader Service. We make a portion of our mailing list available to reputable third parties that offer products we believe may interest you. If you prefer that we not exchange your name with third parties, or if you wish to clarify or modify your communication preferences, please visit us at www.ReaderService.com/consumerschoice or write to us at Reader Service Preference Service, P.O. Box 9062, Buffalo, NY 14269. Include your complete name and address.

H-R-09/11

"You tell her that when she does, Irma will have a cup of tea waiting for her." The woman said goodbye, then headed out of the coffee shop.

"That was nice," Faith said, then grinned. "But a total interruption to finding out about this new guy."

Carrie took a deep breath. "He's a single dad with a little girl who is the most adorable creature in the universe." The details spilled out of her like an overflowing bucket. Her mind was still swimming with the weekend she'd had—the picnic, the afternoon in her kitchen, the cozy meal with his mother. "And he's tall, dark and—"

"Let me guess. Handsome?"

Carrie nodded, feeling like a schoolgirl when a hot blush spread across her cheeks. "Yes, he is. Very."

Faith leaned closer. "So, how'd you meet him?"

"Actually, he came in the shop last week."

"And did he stock up on those fine Uccelli wines, or just the fine Uccelli princess?" Faith grinned and forked off a bite of brownie.

"Neither. He, uh, just wanted to meet me." She hesitated to tell Faith the whole story about him first being interested in her as a story, not a person.

"That's so cool." Faith reached for her iced latte, and stirred at the whipped cream with her straw. "What's he do? If you say he's a doctor, I'm going to want to know if he has a twin brother."

"No, not a doctor." Carrie fiddled with a brownie crumb. "He works for *Inside Scoop*."

"Oh." Faith's nose wrinkled, then she tried to cover the gesture with her hand. "Well, that's…interesting."

Dread coiled in Carrie's stomach. In the past couple of days, she'd done some of her own research on *Inside Scoop*. Everything she'd found about the show had painted it as tacky, sensationalist. In other words, a celebrity's—and a princess's—worst nightmare. She knew Daniel's background was in solid, honest reporting—even if he'd had one very bad day that she'd found on the internet—so she'd told herself that an interview with him wouldn't be useless fluff. But the heavy feeling in the pit of her stomach, made worse by Faith's expression, said otherwise. "Why did you say it was interesting, like it was terrible?"

Faith let out a long breath. "I don't want to rain on your parade."

"Tell me. Please." Better to know the truth now than after she was totally head over heels for Daniel Reynolds.

Too late, her mind whispered. She was already dangerously close to falling head over heels for him. Even as her better sense reminded her that he was a reporter, and thus, not the kind of person she could trust.

Even as all the signs pointed in the opposite direction, she did trust him. There was something about Daniel—maybe it was the love she saw in his face for Annabelle, or the warmth she felt when she was with his family, or how he seemed to have taken a genuine interest in everything about Carrie—that told her he wasn't like other reporters. That he was something more. Something, no, *someone* special.

"I've watched that show," Faith said. "And it's… well, it's kind of exploitive. They always look for the racy angle or the crazy fact to emphasize. They're not exactly hard news. I'm sorry. I wish I could tell you it wasn't. But you never know. Maybe this guy is different. Maybe the show is moving in a new direction."

"I trust him," Carrie said. They'd talked a lot about the princess test after dinner, and as far as she could tell, Daniel was on the same wavelength as she was. "I think it'll be fine. Either way, I think it's time for some chocolate."

"Hear, hear, sister." Faith grabbed her own fork and each of them took a bite of the chocolate dessert. "I love the way you think."

Carrie returned to the lake cottage a little after ten that night. She stayed up for another hour or so, watching a television show that she didn't remember as soon as she clicked off the remote. Her mind strayed between Daniel, what Faith had told her and what she was trying to accomplish here in the U.S.

What she needed was some sound advice. The kind that could only come from home. She calculated the time difference and picked up the phone.

"*Cara!* It's so wonderful to hear from you," her mother said a moment later. Just hearing Bianca's voice, so effusive and warm, made Carrie miss home and her family. "I knew only one person would call me this early in the morning."

"I'm sorry, Mama."

"No, no. You know I like to get up early to watch the sun rise. It is such a magical time."

Carrie could picture her mother, a world away, sitting on one of the castle's balconies with an afghan tucked around her and a hot cup of tea and a stack of cookies on the table beside her. The same way she'd greeted every morning for as long as Carrie could remember. Bianca would be waiting for the sun to rise, and for the birds to begin their day, to take those few moments of golden splendor for herself before beginning her insanely busy day. It was a tradition that Carrie, the only daughter who never slept in, also liked to keep. Many times she'd joined her mother on the wide, cushioned chairs on the balcony. Some of the best, most intimate conversations she'd had with her mother happened in that quiet time between night and day. "I've watched the sun rise every morning since I arrived here," Carrie said. "I'm so glad you told me about Winter Haven, Mama. It is a beautiful place."

"And does your house face the lake?"

The very lake her mother had talked about often, many times with a tinge of melancholy. Her mother had come here shortly after the queen mother's funeral, a particularly difficult time for the whole family, Carrie had heard. Bianca had left Carrie's older sisters with her mother, and taken her first vacation in forever.

Although she loved her home country, Bianca had talked about the tranquility and peace of Winter Haven so many times, Carrie felt like she had been there herself. When Carrie had gone looking for a rental house she'd insisted to the Realtor that she had to have one on the lake, with a view of the water and the eastern sky. "Yes, it does, Mama, just like the one you stayed in years ago. And I watch the sun kiss the water every morning. Just like you did."

Her mother sighed. "I do miss that sight. It was so beautiful."

"You should come for a visit," Carrie said. "You talked about this place so much when I was a little girl, I know you miss it."

"I...I can't. I'm happy here now. In Uccelli." But her words lacked conviction. Was it because her daughter was here, instead of herself? "Is that why you chose that place? Because I talked about it so much?"

"Yes. It sounded like it was a part of you. And I wanted to see what it was all about. And apparently, you were quite popular while you were here," Carrie teased. "I ran into Irma, who used to run the grocery store in town. She said to say hello."

"Irma?" Did Carrie detect a note of alarm in her mother's voice? Then Bianca let out a little laugh. "I remember her. A very sweet woman."

"She said to stop by anytime you're in town."

"That was nice." A pause. "Have you run into anyone else who remembered my visit?"

"A couple people. You were quite memorable it seems." Carrie chuckled.

"I hadn't intended to be." Her mother sighed. "I wish you hadn't gone to that town. Carlita, there are so many other places in America where you could go."

"Why not? It's a wonderful place, just like you said."

"Sometimes I talk too much." Her mother didn't say anything for a moment. "Don't you think you have stayed away long enough, *cara?* Your sister is engaged, and you should be here to help her with the wedding plans. Come home. I miss you."

"Mama, there are no wedding plans. Allegra hasn't set a date yet."

When she'd told Bianca that Winter Haven would be the home for the first wine shop, her mother had been pleased. Proud even. But ever since Carrie had decided to come to America to run the store herself, her mother's attitude had changed. Maybe it was just that her mother missed having her family together. Mariabella was more often in America than Uccelli, and Allegra was consumed with her royal duties. With Carrie out of the country, the castle probably felt very empty.

But her gut told her there was more to her mother's

attitude than that. What, Carrie couldn't name, but there was definitely…something.

"By the way, I've met someone." Carrie couldn't keep the joy out of her voice. It lit the notes of her words, made a smile curve across her face. "A man named Daniel."

"That's wonderful!" She could practically hear her mother beaming on the other end. "Is he nice?"

"He's amazing. Almost too good to be true."

"Is he a commoner, then?"

An understandable question from a mother who would like to see her daughter settle down and start providing grandchildren. "Yes. But I'm not thinking about marriage." *Liar,* her mind whispered. "We barely know each other."

"I only knew your father for a month before I married him. And this year, we'll be married forty years. I can hardly believe it's been that long, or that I'm that old." Bianca laughed. "Sometimes the fastest love stories are the most lasting."

"One thing at a time, Mama. Right now, I'm focused on the wine shop." Carrie dropped onto the window seat. Outside the nearly full moon danced sparkles of light across the lake.

"I know, *cara.* I want all my daughters to do what makes them happy. But I think you have been gone long enough. I…I miss you. That's all."

Carrie smiled. It was as she'd thought. Nothing to worry about besides a mother missing her daughter. "The shop just barely opened. We're already surpassing our sales goals but I think I need to stay a while longer and establish the Uccelli presence in America. Before you can blink, we'll all be home and around the table again, celebrating Christmas."

"I'm looking forward to that," her mother said softly.

"Me, too." Carrie clutched the phone a little tighter, her heart longing for another country on the other side of the world.

"And when you come home, you'll go back to working for the vineyard, yes?" her mother asked.

"I hope so."

"I think you would do a wonderful job."

Carrie snorted. "Tell that to Papa. He thinks I'm going to change my mind."

"He'll come around. He's just concerned, as any father would be. He wants you to be sure of your path. All we've ever wanted is for you to be happy."

"Me, too, Mama." There was a long pause, one filled with love and concern flowing both ways across the phone lines. As much as Carrie loved her work here, she missed her family and her country, too.

"I hate to say goodbye," her mother said, "but I have to give a speech at the annual Women's Club breakfast."

Carrie chuckled. "Still as busy as ever, even when you're not queen."

"The life of a royal never really cuts its ties," Bianca Santaro said softly, with a note of melancholy. "No matter how far you run or how fast you leave."

CHAPTER SEVEN

"I think we have a winner." Daniel grinned, and felt his grin widen when Carrie answered with a smile. "This should work to keep my boss happy, and you."

She sat beside him in his car as they headed back to the shop after a quick brainstorming lunch on Wednesday. "Thank you. I appreciate you working with me on this. So many other reporters would just…"

"Go for the jugular?"

She nodded.

"That's not me," he said, then wondered how true that was. Hadn't he been that kind of journalist before? And wasn't he just waiting for the chance to go back to that kind of work?

His father and grandfather had all been the kind of reporters who never backed down, who did whatever it took to get the story. Daniel had carried on that legacy, and with pride. But now, he wasn't so sure. Maybe it was just being reduced to the "infotainment" ranks. Maybe it was something more.

Like the way Carrie looked at him with such trust in her eyes, and he wanted nothing more than to keep that look there.

Daniel parked his car a block away from By the Glass—because all the nearby parking was taken up by customers. Clearly, the little shop was a rousing success. It seemed as if every tourist in Winter Haven was in there today. And maybe a few from neighboring areas, judging by the number of out-of-state license plates.

"I better hurry up and get in there. We have a couple temps, but I'm sure Faith is going crazy."

"Let me walk you." They got out of the car and headed down the sidewalk. The weather was perfect— a slight breeze danced the fresh scent of the lake in the air, while the sun kept the temperatures at a balmy eighty-five degrees.

When they got inside, he saw that more than a dozen customers filled the small space. Faith was at the register, busy ringing and wrapping purchases. The two temps were on the floor, talking to customers about wine.

"Thanks again," Carrie said. She pressed a tender kiss to his cheek, the kind that he knew would stay in his memory for a long time. "I have to get back to work."

"Dinner later?"

The smile that broke across her face seemed to light the entire state. "Yes."

Daniel stationed himself in the corner, watching Carrie interact with the customers. She was pleasant, her features animated and friendly. She was wearing black capri pants with kitten heels and a bright pink short-sleeved sweater that emphasized her deep brown eyes and long dark hair.

Damn, she was beautiful. And everything inside him wanted nothing more than to kiss her and kiss her and kiss her, until his brain stopped thinking about work and deadlines and his boss's expectations. Until the world closed in to become just him and her. She'd intrigued him, this princess who wasn't a princess, and all he wanted was more of her.

But that would mean opening his heart and taking a chance on love again. He had Annabelle to think of, his job, and adding in a relationship was just one more risk. One he wasn't sure he should take because he hadn't been so good at the relationship thing the first time. If he ended up back in his old job, he'd be repeating everything he was trying to avoid. The what-ifs plagued his thoughts.

He knew he should get back to work. But his feet stayed cemented to the shop's wood floors.

When the shop's bell tinkled, Carrie looked up. Her gaze locked on Daniel's and she smiled. A lightness filled his chest that he couldn't remember ever feeling before and he found himself crossing the room to her, drawn to the flame of her bright personality.

"I don't know," said Carrie's customer, an older woman wearing a nearly neon floral shirt and matching pants. She turned to her husband, a man completely opposite her in appearance. He was tall and thin and wearing head-to-toe beige.

Daniel chuckled. Mr. and Mrs. Miller, his mother's next-door neighbors. Mr. Miller, whom Daniel didn't think had been happy a day in his life, and Mrs. Miller, his long-suffering and very patient wife.

Mrs. Miller turned to her husband. "What do you think, Walter?"

Mr. Miller scowled. "I think I've had enough shopping for one day."

"But do you think our guests will like this wine?"

"I think I'm going to go sit down on the bench outside. Guests. Nothing but a pain in the neck. Serve 'em water, I say." He harrumphed, then turned and left the shop.

Daniel bit back a chuckle. Mr. Miller never had been especially friendly. Daniel remembered many times when he'd complain across the hedge that separated Greta's house from his about silly things like leaves that had blown onto his lawn or a maple that was putting out too much shade, or, once, a rose that had peeked through the hedge and dared to bring beauty to his yard.

Daniel crossed to Carrie, who was clearly trying to be patient with Mrs. Miller. The older woman was still hemming and hawing about her purchase. "I can personally vouch for this wine, Mrs. Miller," Daniel said. "In fact, I enjoyed a glass of the pinot last night."

"You did?" Mrs. Miller asked. "And what did you think of it?"

"I liked the Uccelli wine very much. It's a lighter, fruitier wine with a number of complex notes. I think it'll be perfect for your guests. And a nice conversation piece."

Carrie arched a brow and smiled again. "The bottle I left at the picnic? I didn't know you drank it."

"I wanted to know everything I could about you and Uccelli." When he heard himself say those words, Daniel realized he was in deep. When had that happened? "What better place to start than with the wine you love so much? The ones you helped create with your own hands?"

A blush colored her cheeks. "I'm glad."

"You worked in the vineyards?" Mrs. Miller asked Carrie, surprise in her arched brows.

Carrie nodded. "I did. I started as a little girl, and did almost every job there is to do in the vineyard."

Mrs. Miller harrumphed. "What kind of princess does that?"

"One who wants to do more than wear a crown," Daniel said. "And also one who loves her country and is very proud of its products."

Carrie smiled at him, and in an instant, his world felt brighter, better. "Thank you."

He nodded, then drifted away while Mrs. Miller picked out several bottles of wine. Was this what it felt like to have it all? The girl and the story?

He knew he was compromising himself. Knew his judgment was being colored by his relationship with Carrie. But for the first time in a long time, he didn't care. The mantle of the Reynolds legacy weighed heavy on his shoulders, and he wanted nothing more than to shrug it off.

The other store clerk came up and joined him. "You must be this Daniel I've heard so much about," she said, and put out a hand. "I'm Faith."

He shook with her. "You look familiar. Did you go to Winter Haven High?"

She nodded. "Graduated seven years ago."

"Ah, a few classes behind me."

Small talk out of the way, Faith got right to the point. "Carrie's really crazy about you, you know."

Warmth filled him. And he was sure he was wearing a goofy smile, as if he was fifteen again and found out the girl he was crushing on had secretly been feeling the same way. God, yes, he was surely in deep. "The feeling's mutual."

Faith pressed a paper invitation into his hand. "I'm having a cookout this Friday night. Carrie's coming, and I think you should, too. She said you have a daughter—go ahead and bring her or anyone else you want.

It's just a big neighborhood party. We'll have marshmallows for the kids to roast, and a beanbag toss."

"Sounds great. I'll be there."

Faith said goodbye and headed off to help Carrie complete Mrs. Miller's transaction. As more customers entered the shop, Daniel waved goodbye and headed out the door to work. Maybe a few hours at his desk would get him to refocus. He had a few more details to square up about Carrie before he wrote up his interview questions.

As he made his way back to his car, he felt the familiar vibration of his cell phone. The caller ID displayed the name of the previous editor of the Winter Haven newspaper. Joe Russo had retired a few years ago, moving up to Michigan to spend his retirement days fishing. He'd been harder than heck to track down. "Mr. Russo. Thanks for returning my call."

"It's raining cats and dogs here. First day I've had to be stuck inside all summer. I bet the fish are biting like crazy. Darn rain."

"This shouldn't take long. I only had a couple questions." Daniel had reached his car. He hopped inside, pulled out his notebook and a pen, and balanced the phone on his shoulder. "Were you editor when Bianca Santaro came to town?"

"Sure was. I remember her. A stunningly beautiful woman, not the kind you forget easily."

"I believe it. Her daughter is just as beautiful." Daniel shifted the phone. "I was thinking of comparing the two women's trips. Carlita is here to run the wine shop, but Bianca came for a vacation. Anything you can tell me about her visit here?"

"You mean the stuff I printed...or the stuff I didn't?"

A bell sounded in Daniel's head. "Stuff you didn't print?"

"Twenty years ago, papers were different," Joe explained. "Especially small-town papers. We weren't running around, trying to give everyone their fifteen minutes. We just wanted to report nice, happy stories."

"And there's a not-so-nice story to go along with Bianca's visit?"

"I wouldn't call it that. More a rumor...and a hunch."

The hairs on the back of Daniel's neck stood at attention. He could hear it humming inside him—the secret that could change everything. It was an instinct, one that he'd honed over the years he'd worked as a reporter, and before Joe said another word, Daniel knew one thing.

This was the kind of information that was going to change everything.

By two, Carrie was more than ready for her break. She dropped onto one of the two stools behind the counter and let out a long breath. "That's the busiest we've been since we opened. I don't think I've ever had a day this insane."

Faith settled onto the opposite stool. "Word is spreading about the wines here. That's a good thing."

Carrie pressed a button on the register—after all these days working here, she had finally conquered the dreaded machine—and a quick report of the day's sales printed out on a thin strip of paper. The numbers she saw were more than great—they were incredible. She couldn't wait to call home later today and tell her father and the vineyard manager about the big splash Uccelli wines were making in the U.S. market.

The marketing efforts she'd put in place a few months ago—advertising in local magazines, a billboard on the Interstate next to the Winter Haven exit and a few targeted radio spots—were finally starting to pay back the investment. She ran a mental list of the next things she wanted to do to capitalize even further on the sales surge. She'd order some promotional products like T-shirts, coasters, wine caddies, and she'd hold a wine tasting in conjunction with a local radio station sometime later in the month.

But first, there was dinner with Daniel. Carrie smiled to herself, then pulled a compact out of her purse and touched up her lipstick, then fussed with her hair.

"Ooh. Hot date?" Faith asked. "With Daniel?"

"Yes." She couldn't stop a grin from spreading across her face.

"He is *hot*." Faith put up a finger and let out a long hiss. "Even hotter than he was back in high school. And you know, forget all that stuff I said about the television show he works for. I heard him talking to Mrs. Miller and he seems amazing."

An even bigger smile curved across Carrie's face. "He is, isn't he?"

Faith laid a hand on Carrie's. "I'm so happy for you."

"Thank you. I know this sounds weird, but it's nice to have just a…normal relationship. Like anyone else would have."

"It doesn't sound weird at all," Faith said softly. "And if you ask me, you deserve it. You're a great person, Carrie, and a great catch."

"Thanks." She was grateful to have a friend like Faith during her stay in America. Faith didn't see her as a princess, a foreigner or as anything other than another woman. It was refreshing and freeing and gave Carrie the confidence that she could someday live the very ordinary life she'd been struggling to have all her life.

Maybe an ordinary life with Daniel and Annabelle?

Her mind darted around the prospect, flirted with images of a future with him. Would they laugh every day? Exchange kisses over their morning coffee? Watch the sun rise over the lake?

Maybe. Just maybe.

The bell over the door jingled and a man stepped inside. He was tall and distinguished-looking, with short light gray hair combed back on the sides and deep chocolate-brown eyes. He wore a short-sleeved T-shirt and jeans that fit his still-trim frame snugly. He had the air of a man who would be as comfortable in a boardroom as he would on a fishing boat. He stood in the doorway for a minute while his eyes adjusted to the darker interior.

Faith started to slip off the seat, but Carrie put a hand on her arm. "Stay, take a break. You've worked hard today already. I'll handle this."

Faith settled back on the stool with a contented sigh. "I won't argue with you."

Carrie headed across the shop. She thought of Daniel and their date tonight, and she found herself hoping the customer would finish quickly. "Hello, sir, and welcome to By The Glass. My name is Carrie and I'm here to help you find the perfect wine."

But the man's gaze wasn't on any of the bottles displayed throughout the store. Or the vast collection of wineglasses and decanters. His focus was entirely on Carrie. "You're her."

"Oh, that. Yes, I am," Carrie said, gesturing toward the sign in the front door. "I'm Princess Carlita Santaro. Of the Uccelli royal family, which is where many of our wines are made."

"I've heard it's a beautiful country."

"It is. Full of rocky shores and beautiful homes that date back before Father Time."

The man chuckled, then his features softened. "You are indeed her."

"I am." Just another tourist here to see the local curiosity of the princess. Maybe she could talk him into at least one bottle of the Uccelli wine as a souvenir of sorts. "Now, can I help you find a wine?"

The door burst open and a woman Carrie remembered from the day before came rushing into the shop, heading straight for Carrie. "Dinner party emergency! My husband invited his boss to dinner tonight. What do you have for wines that guarantee promotions?"

Carrie laughed. "I'm sure we can find something, Mrs. Dell." She turned to her male customer. "Why don't you look around for a bit, sir, and if you need any help, please don't hesitate to ask."

The other man looked as if he wanted to say something more, but then he glanced at Mrs. Dell, and he appeared to change his mind. "I'll do that," he said instead and turned to the racks of wine on the wall. Carrie went back to work and never gave him a second thought.

Later, she wished she had paid closer attention. But at the time, she didn't know what one innocuous conversation could cost her.

CHAPTER EIGHT

DANIEL cursed. And cursed some more. He took a long walk around his mother's block, cursing under his breath the whole way. The neighbors undoubtedly thought he was crazy, but he didn't care. He was sitting on information he hadn't expected, and for the first time in his career, he wished he hadn't done such a thorough job on his research.

No matter how he played this in his head, he couldn't see a way that would keep his boss happy, keep Carrie from enduring a potentially humiliating experience and give everyone a happily ever after.

Or even anything close to it.

Daniel had given up on happy endings for himself a long time ago. He'd seen where believing in being happy forever got him—watching his marriage go down in flames, filing for divorce, and then, standing over a grave site and trying to comfort a little girl who couldn't understand why her mother was never again going to tuck her in at the end of the day.

"Is that you, Daniel Reynolds?"

He turned at the sound of his name. "Hello, Mr. Miller. How are you?"

"Terrible." Walter Miller scowled. "My hip's acting up so I can't hardly walk, my arthritis is making it damned impossible to work in my garage and I got a cracked crown." He pushed at his cheek and winced.

Daniel bit back a chuckle. "Well, at least you're in good spirits."

Walter waved off Daniel's words. "Good spirits are overrated."

"Have a nice night, Mr. Miller." Daniel started to walk away.

"Wait."

Daniel turned back. "Did you need something, Mr. Miller?"

The old man scowled again, then pursed his lips, as if speaking the next words came at a great cost. "I wanted to thank you. For helping the wife make up her mind about that wine. That woman is about going to drive me crazy with all her hemming and hawing."

Daniel smiled. "My pleasure."

"And you tell that princess that we enjoyed her wine. It didn't make me sick."

Yes, he could tell Carrie that. The rest, he wasn't so sure about. "I'm sure she'll appreciate that rousing endorsement."

"Whatcha doing featuring the princess on that *Inside Scoop* trash? I saw them advertising it when I was eating my liver and onions tonight."

Daniel bit back a groan. Apparently, Matt hadn't wasted any time getting a preview on the air.

"Why do you work for a jerk like that?" Mr. Miller asked. "I know the guy who runs that place."

"It's a long story."

Mr. Miller glanced over his shoulder at the house behind him. "Myrtle would have my head for talking about my nephew like that."

"Matt is your nephew?"

"My brother-in-law Charles's kid. Turned out just like his father, too. Bunch of 'em give the family a bad name." Mr. Miller cleared his throat. "So, you gonna marry her?"

The question came out of nowhere and left Daniel reeling. "Marry her?"

"I've seen how you looked at that princess. Come on, boy, you look like a man in love."

"Uh, Mr. Miller, I don't think—"

"Let me give you a word of advice." Walter leaned closer. "Marriage ain't easy. Lord knows it's the hardest damned thing I've ever done. But if you do it right, it'll make you happier than you ever thought possible."

"Well, sir, I hardly know her and—"

"What's that matter?" Walter threw up his hands in frustration at Daniel's clear denseness. "You see happiness, you grab it, boy. Lord knows there ain't much of it going around. It's like that wine."

Daniel shook his head, trying to follow the circuitous path of his neighbor's conversation. "What's like that wine?"

"Love." Walter let out a gust of frustration. "At first, you think you don't need it. Just one more damned bottle to clutter up the kitchen counter. But then you buy it, and you know what happens?"

"Uh, no."

"The woman you love is smiling and singing while she's making dinner because you did something nice. I even opened the bottle, poured my Myrtle a glass. *That* is a happy marriage, son. The kind that keeps a man from wanting to tear his hair out."

Daniel chuckled. "Well, that's some advice, Mr. Miller. Thank you."

"Yeah, don't mention it." He leaned in again. "And I

mean it. Don't mention it to Myrtle. She'll be all kissy and huggy if she hears I said something nice."

"My lips are sealed. Have a good evening." Daniel walked away, the echoes of Walter's mutterings about the length of his lawn echoing in the quiet twilight.

By the time Daniel got back to his mother's house, dusk was falling and he hadn't come up with any solutions. He pulled a beer out of the fridge and dropped into a seat at the kitchen table.

"I thought you were having dinner with Carrie," his mother said.

"I canceled." He glanced out the window, his gut torn by his decisions. "I have too much work to do tonight."

"Well, there's leftovers. Would you like some?" He nodded and his mother fixed him a plate. After it was done reheating in the microwave, she laid the meal before him and took the opposite seat. "I know that look. Something's bothering you. Do you want to talk about it?"

"No." He paused. What good had it ever done him to keep things bottled up? To try to run his world single-handedly? The past year had taught him asking for help was a sign of strength, not weakness. "Yes."

Greta steepled her hands and gave him a kind smile. "I'm here to listen."

Daniel laid down his fork, his appetite gone. "I came across some information today. The kind most reporters would kill for. It could change everything with my career."

"But…"

"I haven't used it yet." The paper in his pocket seemed to weigh ten pounds, laden with results of an interview and a few details checks that proved the story the former newspaper editor had told him. "Dad would say I was a fool. He'd be blaring it on the front page."

"Your father was a good man," Greta said. "But sometimes he didn't make good decisions."

"Everyone makes mistakes, Mom."

"These were different. They were the kind of decisions that haunted him." She toyed with the salt shaker. Daniel waited, sensing this was something his mother needed to say, as difficult as it might be. "I've often thought guilt was the real cause for your father's heart attack."

"Guilt? Over what?"

"He always told you about the good stories he wrote. The ones he took pride in. But the ones that bothered him, that haunted him, he kept to himself. I'd see him brooding and try to get him to talk, but most of the time, he didn't want to talk."

"He never told me anything, either." Daniel had always thought his father's distance was a symptom of a frustrated artist. But apparently there'd been more— more that he hadn't said to his son.

"He had one story, about a missing bank teller and a whole lot of money that went missing with her. Do you remember it? It happened when you were about seven."

"Vaguely."

"Your father was bound and determined to find that woman. She was a young mother, and the whole thing scared the community. So your father uncovered every stone he could. He was working around the clock, getting the news in as fast as he could write it. And then…" His mother let out a sigh. "He realized he'd been wrong about almost everything. The teller wasn't some innocent, out there suffering at the hands of a kidnapper. She was a manipulator who had staged her abduction and in the process, planted information that made her boss look like the guilty party. Maybe hoping the attention would focus on that scandal instead of hers."

"She hadn't been kidnapped, if I remember right. She had embezzled a lot of money from the bank," Daniel said. He recalled some of the story, not all, but enough to remember that part. There was something about the young woman meeting up with her boyfriend and her child in Mexico, where she was finally caught by the police.

His mother nodded. "And in the process, the boss's life was ruined. He was completely innocent—all the information had been fabricated—but he never recovered. The paper had moved on to other stories by then, and the truth became a small paragraph at the back of the section. The bank manager committed suicide a few weeks later, and your father…" Greta sighed. "He took that to heart. If he hadn't been so eager to get the story, he told me, he might have paused to think. He was never the same after that."

"And never here." Daniel's words tasted as bitter as they sounded. He remembered his father pouring himself into his work, jetting off here and there in the quest to find the next headline. He fact-checked and re-searched everything ten times over, becoming almost obsessive about the job.

"True. And his absence was one of his biggest re-grets. I think he was gone all the time because he was trying to make up for that one bad story. And because you idolized your father and I don't think he could admit to you that he had made such a bad mistake."

"I wish he had." It would have humanized the elder

Reynolds. And given the two generations a way to connect. "To me, Dad was this distant, mythical person. The perfect reporter. The one I had to live up to."

Greta's hand covered his. "And you did, and then some."

"I don't know about that."

"But I've seen what it's cost you. For a while there, you were more like him than you realized." Her face softened with concern, and she gave his fingers a squeeze. "You don't have to get the story at all costs, Daniel. You don't have to be the top reporter on the show. You don't have to unearth the next big scoop. There are bigger things in life than that."

"Like what?"

"Like being a good father. Being one Annabelle can look up to and respect. Life is about the connections we make, Daniel. Not about the successes we have at work."

"I do that. I make connections."

Greta arched a brow.

"Okay, so I could do a better job at connecting. But…I guess I don't know how." Daniel pushed the beer away. It wasn't really what he needed or wanted.

"Just start with listening." Greta smiled. "The rest will follow."

"I don't know." He thought he'd been listening to his daughter for the past year, and yet their relationship still felt stalled. He thought he'd been listening to Carrie, but when the scoop landed in his lap, the old urge to reclaim his journalistic pedigree resurfaced. Had he been shoving connections aside, and choosing instead career success?

"Do you remember what it was like for us when your father died?" his mother said. "You were nineteen and even though your father's heart attack wasn't my fault, you blamed me. Things were tense between us for quite a while."

He hung his head. "I know and I'm sorry for that. I understand what you went through now."

Her hand covered his. "It's okay. I understood. The point is you do the best you can do for your children and still try to live your life. Family, and the people you love, have to come first. The rest will follow as it's meant to. Don't be afraid of that, Daniel."

"Mom, I can't." He shook his head, and tried to head off the tears brimming in his eyes. "I'm terrified of screwing it up again. My marriage was a mess. My daughter barely knows me and the thought of trying that all over again with someone else…and maybe screwing that up, too?" His voice broke on the last words, and a tear slid down his cheek. "I…I can't."

"If you're always afraid of what's coming around the corner, you're going to miss the great things that are already here, honey." She gave him a gentle pat, then got to her feet.

His mother left the room, and Daniel sat in the darkening kitchen with his thoughts. Two people in a row had given him the same advice—let people into his heart.

Maybe if he started there the rest, as his mother had said, would follow.

CHAPTER NINE

WEDNESDAY wound to a close. After the hectic day, Carrie knew she should be glad Daniel had canceled their dinner plans, but the parts of her that weren't exhausted still missed him. With the princess test coming up tomorrow, she would have felt better to have seen him, and maybe go over their plan one more time.

Ironic, wasn't it, that she was trying to use an event meant to prove her royalness—with the intention of avoiding that designation in the end? All her life, she'd rebelled against her royal life, wanted nothing to do with that. She'd run from the castle every chance she'd had to work in the vineyards, go off with her friends... be normal.

"You nervous about tomorrow?" Faith asked.

"A little. But I trust Daniel. He and I have a plan for that test, and I know he won't do something to embarrass me."

"A good man like that is hard to find." Faith pulled a small mirror out of her purse and touched up her makeup. "Speaking of meeting great men, are you sure you don't mind closing up?"

"Not at all. Have fun on your date." Earlier, Faith had mentioned she was going on a first date with a new guy, and Carrie had told her she should leave a few minutes early to have extra time to get ready. It would give Carrie some time alone in the shop to strategize for tomorrow.

"Thanks. I will." Faith grinned, then grabbed her purse and headed out the door, while Carrie remained behind to finish the day's last few tasks.

She turned the sign to Closed, then headed for the cash register to pull out the day's deposit and run a final sales report. The machine had just started spitting out the tally on one long piece of receipt paper when the bell over the door jingled. "We're closed," Carrie said without looking up.

"I wanted to talk to you."

Daniel. "Hi." A smile curved across her face, then fell. "What's wrong?"

He ran a hand through his hair. "I've been thinking. Maybe you shouldn't do this interview."

"Why?"

"I just think it'd be better if you didn't. Any amount of media attention can open you up to more and…"

She took a step forward. A rush of anxiety raced through her. "What are you saying? Rather, what *aren't* you saying?"

"Nothing. Just…" He let out a breath. "I think you should reconsider the interview. I just hate to see you end up embarrassed."

In a few steps, she had closed the distance between them. She curved into his arms, and when he wrapped himself around her, any nerves she had dissipated. He was here because he was concerned. Because he cared. "How could that happen when I have such a capable reporter interviewing me?"

He stiffened at her words, then jerked out of her arms. "I don't know if I'd use that word to describe me.

I'm not exactly in high demand these days." The words came out soft and sad. Vulnerable.

"Daniel, you're a great reporter. I've seen some of the pieces you've done. And I think the plan you have for this princess test is great. So what would make you think anything else?"

The clock on the wall ticked away the minutes. A passing car danced beams of light over the wine bottles, sending little shimmering sparkles across the wood floor. A long silence filled the space between them. When Daniel finally spoke, his voice was as soft as the light from the stars.

"After my wife died, I kind of lost it for a while. I came in late, missed interviews, forgot appointments. But the real end of my career came on the air." He paused, took another moment before speaking again. "It was the day of my wife's birthday, and I should have taken the day off. It had only been five months since she died, and it was a hard day, especially for Annabelle. She'd been crying almost from the minute she woke up, begging me not to go to work, asking me where her mother was, and it was as if that was the last straw. All the stress from the last few months, all the worries and trying to get through to my daughter, and still work, it all came to a head. I was a mess. But the news still goes on." He let out a short, sarcastic laugh.

"What happened?" She asked the question, even though she knew the answer. But she sensed Daniel needed to tell the story.

"I started the broadcast okay, but then we had this segment, one of those soldiers coming home from the war pieces. We ran them all the time. Heck, I even interviewed a few of the families over the years. But this time, this day, it was too much to see and bear. All that happy reunion stuff, and the tearful hugs with the kids and dad and the wife. I broke down in the middle of delivering the news." He held up a hand before she could say anything. "It gets worse. When my director tried to cut to the other reporter, I got mad. Every emotion I'd had in the last few months came to the surface and I...well, I freaked out on the air. Threw my script across the room, screamed at the weather guy, stormed off the set. On *live* TV. That was the end of my career. The station kept me on for a few weeks, kept me on a desk, but it was out of pity mostly. It was as if something broke that day and I just couldn't get back to where I was. Eventually they let me go. My reputation—and the internet video of that day—haunted me everywhere I applied. It took me all that time just to get this job."

"I know. I saw the video." She gave him a soft smile. "I researched you, remember?"

"You...you saw it?"

She nodded. "Maybe not your finest moment, but anyone who knew what you'd been through would have to understand. And I...I understand."

"But..."

"What you went through had to be incredibly difficult and to go through it on live TV, essentially, even worse. I know what it's like to live with the media eye always on you, and I can only thank God that I've never had a moment where my world was pulled out from under me."

"It's not fun, I'll tell you that." A slight grin had returned to his face.

She gave his hand a squeeze, and the grin widened. "I also think it took a lot of guts for you to pick yourself up and go back into television."

He let out a gust. "I don't know about that. It's called needing a job."

"Yeah, but that job? I knew from the first day I met you, when you called that program 'infotainment,' that you weren't happy there. Why are you still working at a job you don't like?" Since she'd met Daniel, she'd wondered if he was happy at all as a reporter. When she'd watched the videos of his reports on the internet, she'd seen one thing missing from his eyes.

Passion.

She knew that feeling. Knew how it was to keep trying to fit yourself into the wrong compartment. Daniel, she suspected, had yet to see that about himself.

"Because I have a daughter to provide for," he said. "Because I'm a third-generation reporter. And because—"

"Because it's scary to go against what's expected of you." She laid a hand on his arm. "I know. I've done it."

"It's not that easy, Carrie. You don't understand. I have to take care of Annabelle. I can't just up and quit and do something else. This job at *Inside Scoop* is just a way back to the reporter career I had before."

"Isn't that the very career you said distanced you from your daughter?"

He shrugged. "It's the only one I'm good at."

"You can be good at other things."

"You don't get it. This is what I'm good at. Period. And now that I'm here, my daughter has her grandmother, too."

"But not always you?"

"I'm doing the best I can, Carrie. You don't understand how demanding this field can be."

"I understand that you're justifying choices that really aren't justifiable." As she looked at his face and processed what he'd said, she realized a cold, harsh truth. "So all of this really boils down to story first, people second? Your job before…Annabelle? Before me?"

"No. Well, yes, but not the way you think."

She wanted to believe him. But Daniel had just told her, to her face, that he would protect the job at all costs. Was that what tomorrow's interview was really about? Climbing the ladder a little higher, using her pedigree as a stepping stone? Did he really care about her?

Or just his résumé?

Annabelle refused to take no for an answer. Daniel sat on the edge of her bed, wishing his busy daughter would just fall asleep and he could retreat to the living room for a beer and a little misery wallowing.

Carrie had struck a nerve earlier when she'd asked him about what came first, people or the job. He thought of the paper in his hands, the one he had intended to show her. But once he saw her smile at him, he'd decided to leave the paper in his pocket.

The tiny voice inside his head whispered a question he didn't want to answer. Had he kept the information to himself because he wanted the ultimate scoop tomorrow?

"I don't wanna read that one. I wanna read this one." Annabelle thrust the library copy of *The Princess and the Pea* into his hands.

The slim volume seemed to weigh a thousand pounds. He'd tried six other books, trying to divert Annabelle from the fairy tale, but she'd been determined. Daniel glanced down at the cover, at the image of a rather ordinary-looking woman standing outside a castle, her hand raised to knock on the door. In the fairy tale, the woman was revealed to be a princess, the true love of the prince waiting inside the castle. "And they all lived happily ever after," he said quietly.

"Daddy, read." Annabelle settled herself against his arm.

"We've already read this one three times."

"'Cuz it's my *favorite*." She drew out the last word.

His daughter had no idea how this book affected Daniel. How it reminded him of Carrie. He'd met a woman who cared about his little girl nearly as much as he did. Who had worked magic in Annabelle's smile. Who was unlike any woman he had ever known before, and who had given him hope for a future he'd never thought he'd have again.

The paper in his pocket hung on him like an albatross. A good reporter, the kind of reporter his father had been, and his grandfather, would use that information. Would do what it took to get the ratings.

To restore his reputation as a journalist. The brass ring he'd been seeking in the months since his on-air meltdown dangled in his sights. Grab it, and his reputation could be restored. Leave it be and…

And stay where he was.

"I'm tired," Daniel said. He put the book on Annabelle's nightstand. "We'll read extra books tomorrow night. Belle, I promise."

Too late, he realized he'd said the two words his daughter least wanted to hear. The ones that were as empty as a box of air. Hell, hadn't he just done the same thing with Carrie? Just before he'd left, he'd promised her that the interview would be a piece of cake. No surprises, nothing out of left field.

And in his pocket sat a real curveball.

Annabelle frowned, then rolled over, putting her back to her father. She clutched Whitney to her chest. "I don't wanna read anymore."

"Belle—" He reached for her, but she jerked away.

"Night, Daddy," Annabelle said, her voice firm. And sad.

He leaned over and pressed a kiss to her cheek. Belle pretended to be asleep. Daniel left the room a moment later, his heart broken a little bit more.

That night, Carrie drew a sweater around her shoulders and walked down the long stone-lined path to the lake. The cottage glowed warmly behind her, a little beacon waiting for her to return while the moon glowed above, so bright and full it washed the entire lake in white. She drew in the fresh air, letting it fill her lungs for one long second. It was so beautiful here, so peaceful.

Her mother had left her a voice mail today, begging her to come back to Uccelli. It didn't make sense. All her life, Bianca had encouraged Carrie to forge her own path. And now that she was finally doing it, her mother wanted to rein her back into the royal harness?

The same one Bianca herself had briefly escaped more than two decades before?

Carrie's mind strayed to Daniel. If she did return to Uccelli—and eventually she would have to go back—she wouldn't be able to see him or Annabelle anymore. The thought sent a fissure through her heart.

Already, she'd started picturing a future with him and Annabelle. Dared to dream of a life in a little house like this one.

Who was she kidding? She was a princess, not an ordinary woman who could live in this small Midwestern town and sell wine for the rest of her days.

Even Mariabella, who had married an American businessman a year ago, spent half her time in the U.S. and half the time in Uccelli, still answering the royal call from time to time. The media of both countries kept tabs on her, intrigued by the woman who had declined the crown in favor of a more ordinary life.

Maybe there was hope for a middle ground for Carrie, too. A way to have everything she ever wanted.

Daniel had reassured her before he left, promised again that the princess test and the interview they'd do during it would be painless and easy. That he was on her side. She smiled to herself as she walked farther down the path, her arms crossed against the slight chill.

She heard the crunch of tires on a gravel drive, and wondered if the sound was coming from her driveway or one of the other dozen nearby. There was the sound of a car door closing—echoing in the still vastness of the lake—then the crunch of shoes against the gravel. Carrie turned, trying to see where the sound was coming from.

A man was striding down the path toward her. His form looked familiar, but she couldn't place him. She waited by the lake, sure he was a neighbor—at this time of year, all the lakefront properties were rented or occupied—and would veer off toward another house soon. But he didn't. He kept coming toward her, and for a second, she froze. She should run, get back in the house—

"Carlita?"

His voice was deep, gruff. Familiar.

She drew herself up and tried to fight off the quiver of nervousness in her gut. She was here, by the lake, late at night, and alone. Why had she thought a walk would be a good idea? "Can I help you?"

"I'd like to talk to you."

"Listen, if you're a reporter here to do a story on the local princess, I have no comment. Call me tomorrow at the shop."

He had reached the end of the path, and when the moonlight hit his features, she realized why he looked familiar. He was her customer from earlier today—the one who had left when she got busy with another customer. "I'm not a reporter. I just want to talk to you. *Please.*"

"I'm sorry," she said, taking a step closer. "Do I know you?"

"In a way, yes." He put out his hand. "I'm Richard Parker." He paused a beat, then his gaze met hers. "I'm your father."

CHAPTER TEN

DANIEL stood at his desk, staring down at the opened manila folder on his desk. He'd scrawled Carlita Santaro on the tab in his half-legible handwriting. Then he reached into his shirt pocket, pulled out a long piece of paper covered with notes and stuck it on top of the other papers in the file—interviews, photographs, past media stories.

"You ready, new guy?"

Daniel looked up at the sound of Matt's voice. "Uh, yeah."

"Got any juicy facts we can spring on her? It'd be great to get some kind of scandal. That's a real plus in the ratings."

Daniel shut the folder. "No, no scandals."

"Well, bring me one soon, new guy. You know as well as I do that scandal sells TV. So dig up some dirty and get it on the air."

Daniel bristled, and the urge to tell Matt off rose fast and furious in his chest. Then he thought of Annabelle, and of how she had said to Greta just this morning that she loved living here. Loved the town, the animals in nearly every yard, and loved being near her beloved grandmother. This whole past week, Annabelle had been happy and content. He'd finally begun to feel like he was building a bridge with his daughter.

How could he uproot her again?

Annabelle's needs came first. Once he had a few months of work history behind him here, he could move on to another station, to the career he'd had before. But for now, this was the job he had, as much as it grated against his conscience.

Carrie's words from earlier echoed in his head. He glanced down at the paper again. Career? Or people?

People, he decided as he closed the file. A lightness filled his chest, something he'd almost call joy. He might be looking for another job after this, but if it meant feeling like this every day, he'd take it.

"Let's get to work," Daniel said. "We have a princess test to conduct." Then he walked out of his office, leaving Matt behind.

The door to the studio opened and Carrie stepped inside. Daniel's heart caught for a minute, and he forgot to breathe. She'd forgone her usual jeans and T-shirt and opted instead for a knee-length satiny dress in a vivid blue. The cap sleeve top dropped into a soft V in the front, tapered in at her waist, then flared out in a slight bell. She'd paired the dress with black heels that made her calves curve and enhanced her already incredible legs. She'd curled her hair, and the long dark locks lay in tempting tendrils across her shoulders.

"Wow," he said as he approached her. Carrie's warm vanilla perfume greeted him, and made him want to kiss the inside of her wrist, the curve of her throat... anywhere that had been dusted with the fragrance. "You look beautiful."

A smile curved across her face. "Thank you." She ran a hand down the front of the dress and gave it a dubious look. "Although the minute I can, I'm changing back into jeans."

He ached to reach up and touch her, but knew, with the entire production crew and Matt watching, that he couldn't. "You'll look beautiful either way."

If he'd hoped the compliment would make her smile again, he was wrong. Instead, a look of worry shaded her eyes.

"Um, is there somewhere we can talk?" Carrie asked. "There's something I should tell you."

For the first time, he noticed she looked pale. Shaken. What had happened between last night and today? Surely, it couldn't be their conversation. He'd assured her before he left that everything was going to be fine. And now, with that paper securely in the file, it would be. "Sure, let's go—"

"Okay, people, let's get this show on the road." Matt clapped his hands together. The people in the room jerked to attention. "This is airing tomorrow, so we don't have any time to waste. I've got to get it taped, edited and in the can before tomorrow at five. So let's get to work!"

"I really need to talk to you," she whispered to Daniel.

He glanced around the room. The production crew had moved into action. Cameramen slipped behind their cameras, the director settled into his seat in the production booth. "Can it wait? They're getting ready to tape."

Worry creased her brow. "I don't think we should. This is important."

Matt crossed to Carrie and Daniel and inserted himself between them, essentially ending the conversation. Lights flicked on above them, illuminating the set in a flood of white. Matt waved a hand toward the space. "Behold, our set for today."

It wasn't as bad as Daniel had expected, but it still took the cake for Tackiest Set Ever. The entire set had been done in pink and white with ruffles and rhinestones. It glittered like the Las Vegas strip, which paled in comparison to the ornate, overstuffed bright white furniture that filled the small space. Matt had even hung faux reproductions of Italian art on the temporary walls, all framed in thick gold-painted wood.

"I thought you were going to keep the tacky to a minimum," Daniel said. "We talked about how this piece should have some meaning and depth."

"Meaning and depth." Matt chuckled. "Yeah, I'll keep that in mind. If you see any meaning and depth around this place, let me know." Then he headed back over to Carrie and started gesturing toward the set. "Let's go, folks. We're starting with your plan, and doing that embroidery test first. After that…" He shook his head and smiled the crafty smile Daniel had learned to dread. "I think I'll let the rest be a surprise. Get more reactions that way." He clapped his hands again. "Places, people."

A flicker of worry ran through Daniel, but he brushed it off. This was his piece, after all, and he'd set everything up in advance. There were no surprises—because Daniel had made sure not to write any into the script. It was exactly what he and Carrie had agreed upon a couple days earlier. A silly, lighthearted princess test with an opportunity to interview her about the wines and the shop.

"I'm ready," she said to him. "Are you?"

"Definitely. Remember, this is just for fun. I promise, there won't be anything happening that we didn't talk about already."

She let out a little laugh, but it shook a bit. "I'm counting on that, Daniel. Counting on you."

A production assistant took Carrie's hand and led her over to the stage. Matt followed and stood beside her, while the PA affixed a mike to Carrie's dress. When they were done, Daniel miked up, too, and bounded onto the stage. He shot Carrie a grin, but her features remained stony. Maybe she was just nervous.

The instincts that had served him well for so many years of his career told him otherwise. That knot of dread grew in his stomach. As soon as this was over, he would talk to her.

Matt had added a second chair for Daniel, and given him an embroidery hoop, needle and some thread. The whole thing had the fun, silly air that Daniel had wanted. He began to relax. This would go well, and though it wasn't the hard journalism he had built his career upon, it surely wouldn't hurt to show another side of his personality. Might even lead to a job on a morning show. The thought nearly made him laugh out loud.

"Good thing we didn't add a cooking segment to this," he whispered to Carrie.

"Oh, goodness, that would be a disaster," she said, then laughed, a deep throaty sound that nearly took his breath away. "We'd end up starting a fire."

His gaze met hers, those long dark lashes that shaded big brown eyes, and everything in him went hot with desire. Damn. She was beautiful. No, more than beautiful. Stunning. Unforgettable.

"I think we already have," he said, and for a second, he forgot everything around him, and saw only her.

"Ready, folks?" the floor director asked. Carrie jerked her gaze away from Daniel's and nodded. The spell was broken, and the bright lights of reality invaded.

"Okay. Three…two…one." Then the floor director flicked a finger toward them and the cameras started rolling.

Embroidery. What had possessed her to think this was a good idea? Carrie thought as she pricked her finger for the fourth time. She yanked her hand out from under the linen square. "Ouch. Again." The cameras had been filming her clumsy attempts at stitching a flower into the center of the hoop. Thus far, she'd created a messy Z. "Clearly, this is not my greatest skill."

Daniel held up a hoop that had exactly three stitches on it, each longer than the next. He saw her bite back a laugh.

"Not mine, either. Which is probably a good thing." He chuckled, then set the embroidery on the small end table between them. "I take it you didn't embroider a lot while you were living in the castle?"

She nodded. "Not at all. I was too busy doing everything but act like a princess."

Act like a princess? What kind of princess were you, really? The thoughts darted in and sent her stomach rolling. Her memory flicked to Richard Parker, to the bombshell he'd laid on her last night. *I'm your father.*

"Meaning what?" Daniel asked.

"Um, well, I'm more of an outdoorsy girl. I liked camping, horseback riding, even working in the gardens and the vineyards. I wasn't much for sitting around at home." She dropped her embroidery hoop on top of his and relaxed a bit. So far, everything was going according to the plan she and Daniel had concocted.

But even as she sat there, talking about her royal roots, the truth whispered in her mind.

You're not really a princess. You never were.

"And I was, uh," she said, forcing her mind back on track, "definitely not much for quote, unquote 'lady-like' hobbies."

"Sounds like you're a modern princess."

"Yes, I'd say that's correct."

Really? If you're not descended from royalty after all?

Daniel leaned in, his blue eyes wide, inquisitive. She thought of the secret she had kept from him. Would he understand when she told him later?

Her heart fluttered. She realized suddenly why she cared so much about his reaction. About keeping his trust.

Because she had fallen for this man who kept trying to do the right thing with her, with his daughter, with everyone. He was doing his best right now to show her as she was—not mold her into something she wasn't. He knew the real Carrie, and she…

Well, she loved him for it. That knowledge took flight in her heart, but she had to tamp it down, keep it hidden.

For now. Later, she promised with a small smile, she would tell him.

"Tell me, Princess Carlita," Daniel asked, "how would you define a modern princess?"

She thought about her answer for a moment before speaking. "Someone who lives a life as close to ordinary as possible. I don't want to be Rapunzel up in the tower, secluded and away from the people. I want to be…well, like everyone else."

And she was, more than she'd ever realized.

"That quest to have one day follow the other in a predictable pattern," he said. "To find the quiet niche where you belonged, and just…stay there."

She nodded. He understood her, he truly did. She heard it in his voice, and wondered if maybe after all this was over, they'd each find what they were looking for. And find it with each other.

"I can relate," he said softly. "And I think you deserve that, Carrie."

She smiled, unable to keep her feelings for him from showing on her face. "And so do you, Daniel."

"Cut!" Matt's voice cut through the room like a knife. He strode forward and marched onto the set, his face a stony mask. "What the hell was that? Some touchy-feely crap? Just do the test. We'll get a few laughs for the audience, boost our ratings by outing or proving a princess, and that's it. Nothing more. You got it?"

Daniel rose out of the chair in one fast, fluid movement. "This is my piece, Matt. I'll run it the way I want to. That's what you hired me for, after all."

A muscle twitched in Matt's jaw. He glanced over his shoulder at the production crew, all watching the standoff. "Fine. Do it your way. But I get final editing approval." Matt stalked off the stage and waved at his assistant. "Set up for the second test."

A few minutes later, the fake wall had been removed and the stage reordered. A long dining-room table was moved under the lights, set with so many dishes and silverware, barely a few inches of tablecloth showed. Matt stood to the side, smirking, as if he was sure

Carrie couldn't possibly master the table. The floor director counted down again, then gave them the go signal.

Daniel climbed onto the stage and pulled out the captain's chair for Carrie. "Your seat, miss?"

She settled into the chair, and waited while he pushed it into place. Daniel reached forward, shook out Carrie's napkin and laid it across her lap. "Why thank you, kind sir."

"All part of the service." He moved to the seat on her left and laid his napkin across his lap. Across from them, the camera watched everything with its steady red eye.

The truth churned in Carrie's gut. She had to find a way to tell Daniel. Maybe after this, they could go somewhere quiet and talk. She didn't want him to air this piece and then have the truth come out. He'd been nothing but honest with her, and deserved the same from her.

The first course—soup—was brought out by a production assistant who also poured them some wine and water. Daniel, who she knew had dined in several five-star restaurants over the course of his career, as the guest of some of his influential interview subjects, had no problem picking out the right silverware. Carrie, who had been at many a formal dinner before, also chose the right spoon without a problem. On the sidelines, Matt paced.

"Tell me about your country," Daniel said as he reached for a roll and the butter knife. "What is Uccelli like?"

"It's beautiful." A quiet smile stole across her face. "It sits along the coast, and every day is kissed with the scent of the ocean. The castle was built hundreds of years ago, high atop a rocky cliff. It looks out over the country, like a benevolent parent. The citizens are warm and welcoming, and if you visit there, count on making some new friends."

Across the room, Carrie heard the soft click of a door shutting. She couldn't see past the bright lights of the stage, so she returned her attention to Daniel.

"Uccelli sounds like Utopia," he said.

Carrie laughed. "It's not perfect, but it's pretty great."

"Sounds like a wonderful place to visit."

"It is indeed." Her gaze met his and for a moment, she wondered if maybe someday he would visit the country with her or to see her. Because she already couldn't imagine a day when she wouldn't see him.

"What brought you to America?" he asked.

She put her spoon down and crossed her hands on top of each other. "Several reasons. I wanted to experience living in the United States, just as my sister did a year ago. And I wanted to bring the best of Uccelli, of our wines, to this country. We launched a test market here in Indiana in the town of Winter Haven."

"I've heard wonderful things about the Uccelli wines. Rumor has it that the store is doing well."

Outside the range of the cameras, Matt was gesturing at them to keep eating. Assistants stood to the side, holding platters of food, and looking hesitant about bringing them to the table. Carrie ignored them all and focused her attention on Daniel.

But the truth still tossed and turned inside her, and for the hundredth time, she wondered if she'd made a huge mistake by coming here today.

"We've, uh, been very blessed to be welcomed by the tourist community here," Carrie said.

"And I'm sure it helps that a princess from Uccelli, one who has worked in the vineyards herself, is here to answer questions."

She shifted in her chair. Glanced at the camera, then back at Daniel. "I'd like to think the wines would be a good seller, with or without a princess working in the store."

Princess? You mean fraud, right?

She shushed her thoughts. All they did was distract her, and she really needed to concentrate on the interview.

Daniel leaned back in his chair and took a sip of water. "Did you always work in the vineyards?"

"Off and on during my childhood, but it became my full-time job after college."

He chuckled. "That explains why you aren't the embroidery or ball gown type."

She laughed. "Definitely. I love working in the vineyards because it has real results that you can see, measure, taste. I love watching something I tended grow, and become a product that people can enjoy. I've worked in virtually every part of the vineyard, and now I'm here to learn the retail end of the business, while also putting my sales and marketing degree into use."

"Why did you choose Winter Haven as your test market?"

These were the easy questions, the ones she could respond to nearly by rote. She relaxed a little more, releasing the tight knot in her gut. "Winter Haven had all the qualities we were looking for in a test market. It's the perfect small touristy area with a growing interest in wines. People here don't have access to as many of the European wines as a place like, say, Boston or

New York would. These are the very people we want to get excited about Uccelli's product. But mostly, I chose Winter Haven because it's a town my mother spoke of often, and fondly. She had such wonderful mem…" Carrie's voice trailed off. Her mother's memories. Had they all been lies, too? Was the only thing that made this town wonderful a man she'd had an affair with?

Carrie's gaze went to somewhere else, and Daniel was faced with the one thing all reporters dreaded.

Dead air.

"Wonderful what?" he prompted.

"Uh, memories. It's a wonderful town." A flush filled Carrie's face.

Daniel glanced at her. "Are you okay?"

"She's just fine," Matt called out, as he stepped onto the stage.

"What the hell are you doing? Get off the stage." Daniel turned to the camera crew. "Cut!"

"No can do. I told you I had a surprise in store for you two." Matt made a circular motion, telling the camera people to keep rolling.

Daniel jerked to his feet, but before he could say anything, Matt was already talking. What the hell was going on? Daniel had made his plans clear, and now Matt was thrusting his big feet into the process.

"You fail this princess test, *Carlita Santaro,* if that's your real name," Matt said to her, a leer spreading across his face. "Because it turns out you're not really a princess, are you?"

Daniel's gut churned. He saw the piece of paper in Matt's hand. Knew it well. Too well. Why hadn't he shredded it? Why had he left it in the file?

Carrie's jaw dropped. "I…how did you find out?"

Matt clapped a hand on Daniel's shoulder. "Our

intrepid reporter here uncovered the truth. I knew he was hiding something. Too busy working the touchy-feely, I-like-the-princess angle to bring out the truth. Your daddy isn't the king, is he?"

"How could you?" she said to Daniel. Her face paled. She pushed back her chair and got to her feet. "I'm sorry, I…I have to go."

Then she bolted off the stage. Daniel scrambled to his feet and followed after her. Matt screamed at the cameramen to follow their movements, and the trio of red eyes swung around. Lights came on in the studio, illuminating everything.

"Carrie, wait!"

She spun around. "How could you do this? How could you spring this on me on camera? I trusted you!"

"I had no intentions of telling anyone, Carlita. I swear."

"Stop calling me that! I'm not her! I'm not the third princess of Uccelli. I'm not even a Santaro. And you knew that and exploited it. The job first, people second, huh? I thought you were different. I was wrong. So wrong." Then she turned away and took two steps before she stopped. Her jaw dropped and she let out a gasp.

Annabelle stood there, staring at Carrie, disappointment filling her tiny delicate face. Daniel's mother stood behind her granddaughter, a protective hand on Annabelle's shoulder. "You're not a princess?" Annabelle asked.

"I'm…I'm sorry, Annabelle. I really am." Before Daniel could reach her, Carrie ran from the room. The heavy studio door shut behind her with a thud.

Daniel stood on the other side. How had that gone so horribly wrong? He wheeled around. "What did you do?" He resisted the urge to throw Matt out the window, and instead clenched his fists at his sides.

"I told the story you were too afraid to tell. *'Inside Scoop*'s Princess Test Exposes Fake Princess.'" Matt put air quotes around the words. "Oh, that's going as the lead story. I can't wait to have CBS calling me for footage of our little fake princess exposé."

"You can't do that. You're exploiting her for ratings."

"And? What's wrong with that? It's what the people in our industry do every day."

"Not me," Daniel said. His disgust with his job, with this boss, with the entire production, had reached epic proportions. This wasn't who he was. Wasn't the kind of man he wanted to be. "Not anymore."

"Right. Like you wouldn't have sacrificed your right arm to have a story like this when you worked in New York. Why you shoved that little tidbit into a file instead of using it, I'll never know. That was pure ratings gold."

"The other Daniel Reynolds, the one I used to be, would have used it. That one made a lot of mistakes over the course of his life. But this Daniel Reynolds says…I quit." He threw up his hands and for the first time since he'd come to work at *Inside Scoop,* he felt good about himself. "I'm not that man anymore. And I'm tired of pretending I am."

Then he gathered two of the three people who meant the most to him in the world—his mother, his daughter, one holding each hand—and walked out of the studio.

CHAPTER ELEVEN

THE window seat offered no comfort. After leaving the studio, Carrie had come back to the rental cottage, curled up with a glass of iced tea and a blanket, and instead of feeling relaxed, she felt tense, nervous. Anxious.

But most of all, distraught that Annabelle had to see that scene today. If Carrie had known the little girl was there, she never would have said anything. What a mess. And worse, one she'd caused all by herself. First, by agreeing to that crazy princess test, and second by blurting out the one thing she'd wanted to keep quiet.

She thought she'd tamed that impulsive streak of hers. That finally, here, working in the shop with her future at stake, she had learned to think first and act later. Apparently not.

Daniel had tried calling her twice already, but she'd let the calls go straight to voice mail. He was a problem she didn't want to deal with. Not now.

Chances were he only wanted his follow-up interview anyway. The one where he got the truth about her parentage, then broadcast it to the world. She closed her eyes, already seeing the future ahead. The wine shop would maybe survive, but she had no doubt sales would drop. And Uccelli wines would forever be tainted by their relation to her. Not to mention how her parents were going to react.

She sighed. Toyed with her cell phone, turning it over and over in her palm.

It was time.

The call seemed to take forever to connect. Carrie's thumb danced over the disconnect button once, twice, three times. But in the end she waited for the ring and the familiar greeting.

"*Mia bella!* What a wonderful surprise!" Her mother's voice was warm, full of love and for a second, Carrie considered making this a purely social call. But she couldn't. She needed answers.

"Hello, Mama." Carrie fiddled with the fringe of the patterned afghan. It took a moment to get the next words past her throat. "I met someone else in Winter Haven. Someone who knows you."

"You did? How nice." Her mother's voice had gone flat. Tension winnowed the thousands of miles between them to mere inches.

"He said he knew you. Knew you quite well. Do you remember a man named Richard Parker?"

"Richard." Bianca expelled the name in one long breath. "He contacted you?"

"Yes. And he told me that…" Carrie closed her eyes and she was back there by the lake, seeing a familiar gaze that was so like her own, hearing again the words that changed everything. "That he's my father." A sob caught in her throat. "Is it true?"

Her mother didn't say anything for a long time. The phone line hissed between them. "Yes."

One word, and it changed everything Carrie thought she knew about herself. She didn't realize it until that moment, but she'd been hoping her mother would refute the claim. That Richard was crazy or that Carrie had imagined the whole thing. The phone trembled against her ear, and tears slid down her cheeks. "Why didn't you tell me?"

"I never thought he'd know. I left so fast, and I...I never talked to him again. And it was easier to go back to my life and forget it ever happened."

"He said he knew all along. And he was sure that was why you left America so quickly. But when you chose to go back to Uccelli, to Papa, he knew the best thing he could do was stay away." At first, when Richard Parker had come to her with his story, she'd wanted to think he was lying. That he was some gold digger just looking to blackmail the royal family.

But as they'd talked, and one hour of conversation stretched into two, she'd realized this was a man who deeply loved her mother and always had. He had only told Carrie who he was because he'd thought she was old enough to know the truth. And because he wanted to know his daughter.

"He never contacted me again," Bianca said softly. "I always wondered how he was."

She could hear her mother's love in her voice. The affair may have ended two decades ago, but clearly, the affection had never completely died. That tempered Carrie's anger about not being told the truth. Some. "He eventually married. Had two kids of his own. He's still living in the area, still working in law. But he's older now, of course, and thinking about retiring."

"That's good," her mother said. A note of melancholy sounded in her words. "I'm sorry you had to find out that way. I never intended to say anything."

"I had a right to know, Mama."

"I'm sorry, *cara.* I truly am."

"Does Papa know?"

"Yes." Her mother let out a long breath. "I almost left, you know. Almost abdicated, gave up everything."

"You would have left Mariabella and Allegra?"

"No, never. But I wanted more. I wanted…what I didn't have. Ironically, Richard was the one who made me see what the right choice was."

"And so you stayed." Carrie didn't know if that made her angry or made her sympathize.

"My place is here, *cara*. With the man I truly love, and the country I love. I didn't realize how much I loved your father and Uccelli until I almost lost it all."

Carrie had liked Richard Parker. He had an easy way about him that was the complete opposite of her stubborn, passionate and loving father. She could see why her mother had liked him, too. Richard was the placid lake she looked out over, the quiet in the middle of the ocean that was the royal life. "I wish you had told me. All these years, and I never had a chance to get to know him."

"I'm sorry. For so many reasons." Bianca's voice held true contriteness and massive regret.

A lump formed in Carrie's throat. "I have to go, Mama. I just…need some time to think about this."

"I love you, Carlita. I was only doing what I thought was best."

"And so was I," she said quietly, thinking of what had happened in the studio today, how she had left instead of standing up to the claim. "But I'm not sure I did that."

After they finished talking, Carrie stayed curled up in that window seat for a long, long time, watching the moon sparkle on the lake and listening to the night birds call to each other.

* * *

Annabelle refused to talk to him. She'd curled up in her bed and turned toward the wall, away from him, and pretended to go to sleep. When he'd invited his mother and Annabelle down to the studio to see the taping of the princess test, he'd thought it would be something Annabelle would enjoy. Never in his wildest dreams had he thought Matt would drop the bombshell about Carrie's real identity and leave his daughter confused—and angry with him for letting her down.

Again.

It was his own fault for leaving that paper in the file. He should have found a way to head that off, to stop the bomb before it exploded. And ruined Carrie's life. This was worse than the internet-publicized moment, because this time, the aftershocks of his actions had affected the people he cared about.

"Want me to read a story?" he said, trying again with Annabelle.

A muffled, "no."

"Uh…how about a game of Candy Land?"

"No."

He racked his brain for something else. Came up nearly empty. "Do you want me to get your blankie?"

She rolled back to look at him. "Daddy, I don't have a blankie anymore. That was when I was a *baby.*" She sighed with a gust of air, and then turned back to the wall.

He was tempted to walk out of the room. Always, it had been easier to do that than to tear down the walls between himself and his daughter. Because opening those walls meant opening old wounds, some that were still healing.

He took a half step toward the door, then turned back. *Just start by listening.*

Was that what he'd been doing wrong when it came to his daughter, too? He'd been so busy working and trying to keep their heads above water that he'd stopped listening? He looked at her delicate, precious face, pressed against the pillow, eyes closed but eyelashes fluttering as she peeked to see if he'd left.

Listening to Annabelle meant entering her world. Something he had waited far too long to do. Clearly, because he was missing the details about what was important to her. He'd already lost his wife—he couldn't lose his daughter, too. And maybe, if he could fix this part of his life, he could find a way to fix things with Carrie, too. One person at a time.

He crossed to the corner of her room and lowered himself into one of the tiny chairs that ringed Annabelle's play table. He sure hoped this thing could hold his weight.

Then he reached for two of the stuffed animals she kept in a bin nearby, plopped them into two other chairs, and began to talk. "Welcome to my tea party, Boo-Boo and uh…Rabbit." Shoot. He still didn't remember that one's name. "Who wants tea?"

He heard Annabelle roll over. But she didn't speak or get out of bed. He forged forward, feeling silly, but knowing more was at stake here than his embarrassment level. "Okay, Boo-Boo, here you go." He picked up the plastic pot and pretended to fill the matching cup. "Oh, and a cookie, too? Just one, though, or you won't have room for breakfast."

Out of the corner of his eye, he saw Annabelle sit up. Swing her legs over the side of the bed. Hope leaped in his chest.

"Now, Rabbit, you have to wait your turn." He pretended to fill another cup, raising his voice to an even more exaggerated level. "Nope, no carrots today. Sorry, buddy." Then he turned the pot toward a third cup. "What do you guys say we pour Annabelle a cup? In case she decides to join us." The stuffed animals stared back at him, mute. Like they thought he was an idiot.

Part of him felt like one, but the other part, the side that hadn't known about Belle's blankie, and had been staring at the back of her head tonight, told him to keep going. Miracles didn't happen overnight.

He pushed the third cup in front of the empty seat, then made a hissing sound as he "filled" his own. He smacked his forehead, then leaned toward Boo-Boo. "Guess what I forgot? To get dressed up for the tea party. You can't go to a tea party in your regular clothes. Annabelle told me that and I forgot. How silly am I?" He got to his feet and turned toward Annabelle's bin of dress-up clothes. "Wow, guys, what should I wear?"

"Wear this, Daddy." Annabelle thrust a pink feathered boa into his hands. It was silly and garish and exactly what his daughter wanted, and that, Daniel realized, was what he wanted, too.

"Perfect." He took the boa, flipped it around his neck, then sat back down. It fluttered against his chest, all girly, and exactly what his daughter wanted. He allowed that hope in his chest to take flight, to dare to believe this could all be fixed. Maybe not with one tea party, but it was a start. "Are you going to join us, Princess Annabelle?"

She nodded, then slipped on her tiara and her plastic shoes and climbed into her chair. "Yup. I love tea parties, Daddy."

He smiled, and captured her chin in his hand. "And I love you, baby."

A smile winged its way across Annabelle's face. Her eyes glimmered. "Daddy?"

"Yes?"

"I love you. Lots." Then she sprang out of her chair and into his arms. And filled Daniel's heart.

CHAPTER TWELVE

THE next day, the shop was her saving grace. Carrie poured herself into work, and it helped keep her mind off what was to come later that day when the TV program aired. After that, there'd be no peace, not for her. The rest of the world's media would descend, and there would be nothing but negative headlines for months to come.

And caught in the crossfire would be her beloved vineyard.

"You're pretty quiet today," Faith said, coming up beside Carrie.

"Just thinking about what's going to happen when that segment airs today." When she arrived at work Friday morning, she'd told Faith about the debacle in the studio. Faith had been understanding and compassionate—a true friend.

"It may not be as bad as you think." Faith clasped Carrie's hand. "Okay, maybe it will. But you're a strong person. You'll be fine."

"I hope so."

Faith gave Carrie's hand a squeeze. "You know, if you're going to run a vineyard, you need to be more sure about things."

"The vineyard and the wines we produce are perfect. I'm sure about those."

"I meant sure about *you*." Her green eyes met Carrie's. "You're amazing at this, and you're going to be amazing running the vineyard or the American operations or whatever part of the business you take on."

"Sales are high because people are impressed by the princess being here." She pursed her lips. "Though now that people will find out that the princess isn't really a princess after all, I'm sure sales will drop."

"Yes, some people bought the wines just because they were affiliated with royalty. But most of our sales—and our repeat customers—have been here because the wines were amazing, and you are an amazing salesperson. I've learned a lot just by watching you."

"You have?"

"You listen to people. You engage them. And you give them advice, not try to make the hard sale. I can tell the customers really appreciate that. So it's not because you're a princess, it's because you're a *person* first."

All her life, Carrie had floundered around, trying to find where she fit in the world as someone other than the third princess of Uccelli. And now, here in this little shop, she had found her place. She was just Carrie, a woman passionate about her job.

And she had been successful at being herself. The feeling was a new one, and made her heart swell. If only there was a way to preserve that and her family's reputation at the same time.

The shop door opened and Daniel stepped inside. For a second, Carrie's pulse raced, then she reminded herself that he was part of the television show that was about to ruin her life in a few short hours. He'd been the one to unearth those facts; he'd been the one to use them against her. She turned away and headed into the back room. "I can't deal with him," she said to Faith.

If she hoped that Daniel would take that as a hint and leave her be, he didn't. Instead, he followed behind her seconds later. "You got your story, Daniel. Just leave me alone."

"That wasn't the story I wanted. I had no intentions of using that information on the air."

"Really? Didn't you tell me the whole idea was to prove whether I was a fake princess? And when you came across the information about my real father, why didn't you come to me?"

"I…" He sighed. "Okay, yes, for a while I did consider using it. But then I thought about what such a revelation would do to you, to this business, and I chose not to tell anyone."

"Then how did Matt find out?" She put up her hand before he could answer. "You know, it doesn't even matter. I hope you make millions blasting that scandal all over the world."

He let out a low curse and shook his head. "I had no idea things would turn out that way."

"Maybe not. But how convenient that it's all on tape. Story first, people second. Right?"

"Digging up the truth is my *job,* Carrie."

She refused to feel bad. To let him soften her. "You can get another. One that lets you sleep with your conscience intact." She turned away, busying herself with a stack of paperwork on the desk.

"Carrie—"

"You have your scoop." She waved at the door. "Go blast it to the world, Daniel."

"Is that the kind of man you think I am?" When she didn't answer, he took her arm and gently turned her toward him. "Do you really think that's what I wanted?"

"What reporter doesn't want the big scoop?" She shook her head, refusing to shed the tears brimming in her eyes.

"I used to," he said. "I used to live for the adrenaline rush of landing that elusive interview, chasing after the facts, hunting down the truth. But where did that get me? Widowed and raising a daughter who can't trust me. And losing the one woman who truly understood me." His voice broke on the last few words, and Carrie's resolve stumbled.

Which Daniel was he? The one who wanted the story, no matter the personal cost? Or this fractured man who was merely trying to do the right thing?

There was a soft knock on the door and Faith popped her head in. "Carrie, I hate to interrupt, but there's someone here asking for you. It's a repeat customer with some questions about wines."

"I have to go," she said. "You can let yourself out the back." She gestured behind her, then left the room before her weakened resolve finally shattered.

It took about thirty seconds for Daniel to decide what to do. He stood in the alleyway behind By the Glass, half tempted to go back in there and camp in the display case until Carrie believed him. But even after only a couple of weeks, he knew her, and knew words wouldn't be enough. A woman like Carrie who had grown up to see the media as the enemy would need tangible proof of his words.

If he was going to produce that, he was going to have to hurry.

He hopped in his car and hurried down to the studio, almost breaking the land-speed record. When he got to the building, he hesitated outside the locked studio entrance. He punched in the entrance code, then breathed a sigh of relief. Matt hadn't had time to change the number yet.

He glanced at his watch. Two hours until airtime. He needed to find a way to get in there and accomplish a miracle.

His code worked for the production booth, too, and he exhaled another bit of relief to find only one person inside the equipment-filled room. "Hey, Ted. How's it going?"

Ted Lynch, a twentysomething self-professed geek who had worked at the studio for a year, spun around in his chair. "Daniel? I thought Matt fired you."

He could play this one of two ways. Lie or tell the truth. He tried to assess Ted, but he'd only known the guy a few weeks. Not nearly long enough to know if he was going to call security or let Daniel at the controls. "You know Matt," Daniel said, testing the waters. "Tough guy to work with."

Ted snorted. "Definitely."

"What do you think of this princess test thing?"

"Honestly?" Ted looked around the room even though they were the only ones there. "I think it's stupid. I spent all those years in college to get out in the world and make a difference. Make a statement, you know? And what does this say?"

"Nothing good," Daniel said. He dropped into another swivel chair and spun it toward Ted. "I have a way to make a statement, if you're game."

"How?"

"Well, it's a little risky." *A little?* his mind screamed. *Try a lot.* "And it might get you in trouble. Or in the best-case scenario, win you an Emmy."

Excitement rose in Ted's eyes, flushed in his face. Relief flooded Daniel. He hadn't been sure until just then that Ted wouldn't call security. "What kind of trouble?" Ted asked.

"The best kind." Daniel pulled his seat up, cued up the segment they'd taped yesterday and got to work.

Fifteen minutes before the episode of *Inside Scoop* was due to air, Faith convinced Carrie to close up shop and go home. "And after you watch it, come on over to my cookout. You'll be glad you got out of the house."

"Thanks. I will." She gave Faith a quick hug, then headed out the door and back to the quiet lake cottage. She opened the door and stepped inside, but this time, the cozy little house didn't fill her with the same sense of peace it usually did. The empty space felt…lonely.

She poured a glass of Uccelli red, then curled up on the sofa and flicked on the television. As much as she didn't want to, she should watch the *Inside Scoop* debacle. Forewarned was forearmed, and she knew she needed to arm herself as well as possible for what was coming next.

But as the logo for *Inside Scoop* started to spin into view, her courage faltered and she shut off the television. She got to her feet, grabbed a light denim jacket to ward off the slight evening chill and headed outside. Faith lived only a half mile away on the other side of the lake, and Carrie opted to walk the distance rather than drive. The fresh air felt cool against her hot face and helped clear her head. A little.

The scent of roasting hot dogs and hamburgers drew her down Faith's driveway, around her cottage and into the lush green backyard. Several people Carrie knew were already there, as well as a few she didn't.

Her gaze scanned the crowd for Daniel, then she chided herself for even caring where he was. Chances were, he was at a bar in town, toasting his new success.

She considered turning around. It would be so much easier to retreat into solitude, to deal with Daniel's betrayal while sitting alone in the window seat of her cottage.

The old Carrie, the one who had been taught to avoid public displays of emotions, the one who had learned the hard way that few friends were true friends, would have done just that. Or she would have run off on some crazy last-minute trip to avoid dealing with reality.

But the new Carrie, the one who craved normalcy, stayed. Normal people went to their friends when they had a problem. Normal people went to cookouts and let the good food and good company help them forget for a little while. And from here on out, Carrie was going to be normal—

Whatever that encompassed for her. No more running from her heritage. No more running from her family's expectations. No more running from herself.

Faith came over to greet her. "Hey, you're here earlier than I expected. Did you catch the show?"

Carrie shook her head. "I couldn't. I didn't want to see my life fall apart on television."

"Maybe it wasn't that bad."

"And maybe it was worse. Anyway, I think I need something fattening and bad for my arteries."

Faith laughed and led Carrie toward the group sitting in lawn chairs around a fire pit. "Well, you came to the right place for that."

Two cheeseburgers and a huge handful of potato chips later, Carrie had mastered relaxation, or at least the art of looking relaxed. She sat back in the webbed lawn chair, sipping a glass of Uccelli red, and chatted and laughed with the people around her. Some had been customers, others were Faith's friends and neighbors, but all of them greeted her warmly and treated her like just another neighbor.

But inside, her stomach churned with the knowledge that her world had imploded a little while ago, and everything she had worked so hard to build would be destroyed. Her cell phone sat heavy in her pocket. Any second now, she expected it to ring. The only question was whether the national media or her father would call first.

When her cell phone rang, she excused herself, moved to a quiet corner of the yard and flipped it out. It was the middle of the night in Uccelli, but she wasn't surprised. Her mother might be the early bird, but her father was the night owl. He preferred, he said, to get his work done while the rest of Uccelli was asleep—and thus unavailable to interrupt him. "Hello, Papa."

He didn't waste time on small talk. "I talked to your mother. And I know you found out the truth about your biological father."

She had secretly hoped some miracle would come along and erase what had happened. But it didn't, and now they had to face the truth. She couldn't delay any longer in telling her parents the whole story.

"I'm so sorry, Papa. When he came to talk to me, I had no idea who he was." She didn't want to hurt her father. She loved him, and knew this had to be a hard conversation. She wished they didn't have to have it at all, but deep in her heart, she knew talking about it was better than keeping the information buried any longer.

"No, it is good that you know. That you met him. He has a right to know you, as well. We should have told you a long time ago, but it's the sort of thing that is hard to find words to say."

"I know, Papa." She bit her lip and forced herself to tell her father the rest. "There's a television show here that interviewed me, and one of the reporters there exposed the truth. They were supposed to air it tonight, which means the media will come knocking any second now."

She waited for the explosion that was sure to come. Her passionate father had never hesitated about letting her know his opinions on her mistakes. The times when she'd opted out of a family appearance to go racing horses across the fields with one of the staff. Or sneaked off in the middle of a ceremony and taken a taxi back to the castle. Even when she was little, and fidgeting through every castle event, he'd been the one to admonish her.

"We will deal with that when it hits the wire services," he said. "Perhaps it is better that the truth is out there."

"How can it be? It'll smear the family name, and that will hurt the vineyard."

"Perhaps. Or perhaps it will show people that even a queen can be human. I forgave your mother a long time ago, *cara*. The pressures of this job and the eyes of the public are like a vise that wrap around your life. They shackle you, and I cannot blame her for wanting a small moment of escape." He paused a second. "I can't blame you, either."

"I was never a good princess, Papa. You were right all along. I should have taken my royal life more seriously. Settled down on a career a long time ago."

"No, my dear, you were the perfect princess." His voice softened. "This is a difficult life and I only made it more difficult for you. One would think I'd have learned my lesson with your sister, but when you're a parent and also king, it is hard."

"You did fine, Papa."

He laughed. "Even I know I was too hard on you. I merely wanted you to have the strong foundation you needed to survive this life. To blossom within the bounds of royalty."

"And all I did was run from that as often as I could. And try out nearly every career in the world."

"If you ask me, you did the smartest thing. You lived as normal a life as you could. And perhaps in the coming years, that will stand you well. Give you the tools you need to handle this life."

Surprise filled Carrie. "I think it will, Papa."

"Now that you have had your taste of the world, are you going to return to Uccelli? Or stay there and run the American operation?"

He was offering her everything she'd ever wanted—the job, the freedom, the support. What she had worked for, what her heart had wanted.

The operative word was *had,* though. She glanced up and saw a pair of figures round the corner of Faith's house. One tall, one short and petite. Carrie caught her breath and tried her damnedest to look like she didn't care. But she did. Very much.

Especially when she realized the new guests were Annabelle and Daniel's mother. And not Daniel.

Stay here, in America, and have everything she

wanted—except one thing. "I don't know, Papa. Perhaps it would be best if I returned to Uccelli."

"The choice is up to you. Either way, I want you working for the vineyards. I have seen the sales reports, Carlita, and I am very proud of the work you have done."

She basked in his praise. The validation felt good. Damned good. "Thank you."

"I admit, I was a little stubborn when it came to the vineyards. I should have trusted that you knew what you wanted."

She laughed. "I didn't know what I wanted for a long, long time so it's no surprise that you were a little leery about that. But I know now, Papa. I love the vineyards. Love bringing Uccelli's wines to the world."

"Then that is what you shall do."

"Even if I'm no longer princess?"

"You will always be my daughter, *cara*. And you will always be a princess to me. Always." His words were soft and emotional, filled with honesty, and brought tears to Carrie's eyes.

"Oh, Papa, I love you." Her voice broke, and a happy sob caught in her throat.

"I love you, too, Carlita." His words were gruff, telling her that her stalwart father had a tear or two in his eyes, too.

The words bridged the thousands of miles between them. Richard Parker might be her biological father, but the father of her heart, the one who loved her more than anything in the world, was Franco Santaro. Princess or not, she knew she would always be one in his eyes, and he would always be the king of everything in hers. "I love you," she whispered again to her father, and their rocky relationship finally began to smooth.

CHAPTER THIRTEEN

"Princess Carrie!" Annabelle burst into a run and plowed straight into Carrie's arms. A few feet away, Belle's grandmother brought up the rear behind the fireball of Annabelle. "I missed you!"

Carrie's heart melted. She bent down, wrapped her arms around Annabelle in a tight hug. "I missed you, too, Princess Annabelle."

The older woman shook hands with Carrie. "It's nice to see you."

"Same to you." Carrie smiled. In another life, she suspected she and Greta would have gotten along well. She seemed like the kind of warm woman who would make the perfect mother-in-law.

In another life. With another woman. Because she and Daniel were done.

"I was so busy this week," Annabelle said, with an exaggerated whoosh of exhaustion. "I practiced my princess walk, and I played with Whitney, and Grandma helped me make brownies, and then last night, when I was supposed to be asleep, Daddy came in and…and he set up a tea party!"

"He did?"

"Uh-huh. And Daddy came to the party, and Boo-Boo came and Bunny Boy, too. Whitney didn't come 'cuz she was sleeping. But Daddy and I had fun. I wore my princess crown and my stick shoes."

"Sounds like a wonderful time."

"Daddy looked silly." Annabelle giggled. "Even Boo-Boo laughed."

So Daniel had finally found the right recipe for a tea party with his daughter. The thought warmed Carrie's heart, and for a second, she pictured the three of them seated around a table, feigning tea drinking and sandwich nibbling. Then she jerked herself back to reality. She wasn't going to be with Daniel. Not now. Not ever.

Because in the end, he had chosen his career over her. And as much as she might enjoy being a part of Annabelle's life, she couldn't have a relationship with a man she couldn't trust.

When Carrie sat down on the picnic bench, Annabelle clambered into her lap, and when she did, Carrie realized she had made a connection with this girl. One that would last for a long time, perhaps forever.

Carlita Santaro, the wild child who had done her best to not be tied down to her home, her family or anything else in her life, was permanently tied to this little girl. She couldn't imagine going back to Uccelli and not seeing Annabelle's bright, impish face every day. Or not hearing the dozens of questions the inquisitive girl threw out like bread crumbs.

She was connected. She, the woman who had never wanted to settle down, to have her life forever linked with someone else's, now felt a keen sense of loss knowing that she had found something incredible and had to let it go. The thought sent tears rushing to her eyes. "Annabelle, I, uh, need to get a drink of water. Do you want to wait here with your grandmother for me?"

Annabelle nodded. Carrie scrambled to her feet and headed away from the group, seeking solace in the dark stand of trees at the back of the yard.

Then she saw him, and her thoughts froze. Daniel stopped by the picnic table, greeted his mother with a kiss on the cheek, then stopped when she said something to him. He looked up, his gaze skipping across the guests before coming to rest on Carrie across the yard.

Heat roared through her veins. She cursed the reaction and tried to find something—anything—to do besides watch Daniel cross the lawn toward her. To fight the anticipation swelling inside her. She diverted from her path and headed back to the fire pit. A roasting stick rested against the chair on her left, and she grabbed it, then poked a marshmallow onto the end and leaned forward, feigning great interest in toasting the white pouf of sugar.

"I was hoping the fire wouldn't be going."

She glanced up at him, even as she cursed herself for doing so. "Why?"

A grin curved across his lips, and her traitor heart skipped a beat. "Because then I could have impressed you with my amazing Boy Scout skills."

"Well, the fire *is* burning. And if I don't watch this, so will my marshmallow." She jerked her attention back to the stick where a blackened blob now sat instead of the marshmallow.

"I think it's already past saving." Daniel picked up another roasting stick, one with two prongs, and slid a pair of marshmallows onto the ends. "The trick is to keep it away from the flame and just let it toast gently over the hot coals. Keep an eye on it, turn it often, and before you know it, you'll have what you wanted."

"If only it were that simple." She tossed the ruined treat into the fire, then put her roasting stick aside.

"It *is* that simple, Carrie." He pulled the stick back, then held it out to her, displaying a perfectly golden-brown marshmallow on the end. "For you, milady."

She wiggled the sticky dessert off the end and popped it into her mouth. The sugar melted against her tongue, sweet and perfect. She tried not to compare it to kissing Daniel, to hearing his deep voice when he spoke her name—but she failed. "Uh, thank you."

Daniel ate the second one, then put the stick back, brushed off his hands and got to his feet. "Can we talk?"

She should say no. She should stay right here and talk to the other guests. She shouldn't go anywhere with Daniel Reynolds. "I should…"

She couldn't finish the sentence because she didn't know what to do. More, what she *wanted* to do. Instead, she let the indecision waver in her voice.

"Please come with me. I have something I need to tell you." He put out his hand, and before she could think twice, she put her palm in his.

She released him as soon as they started walking. She didn't want to fall into the trap of caring about him, of trusting him again. But as she walked away and heard Annabelle's lyrical laughter echoing in the yard, her heart ached with a pain that ran bone-deep.

They walked in silence for a little while, until they reached a low-slung swing that Faith had set up under a willow tree. The graceful branches danced in the slight breeze and formed a soft golden canopy over the swing. Dusk was beginning to fall, giving the tableau a cozy, intimate feel. Across the yard, people talked and laughed, their voices creating a rhythmic melody.

Carrie took a seat on the swing, but Daniel remained standing. He gripped one of the bars, and smiled down at her. "God, how I've missed your beautiful face."

She sighed and got to her feet. "Don't."

"Don't what?"

"Act like everything's fine when we both know it isn't." She started to walk away, but he grabbed her hand and tugged her back to him. She collided with his chest and wanted so badly to curve into that warm strength, to inhale the dark notes of his cologne and to lift her mouth to his. Instead, she turned away, and broke the contact.

"I'm sorry. Maybe I shouldn't have led with that. But I have missed you." Daniel didn't release her. He waited until her gaze met his. "Everything is going to be fine, Carrie. I promise."

"Maybe for today. I know you're just waiting to drop that bomb, Daniel. Maybe you're waiting until you find my real father and drag him in for an interview. Or maybe until you have a chance to fly to Uccelli, ambush my parents and get their reactions." Panic rose in her throat and arched the pitch in her voice. She could feel her fragile world, one so newly constructed it still seemed to have the wrapping on it, collapsing around her. She'd barely had a chance to prove herself with the Uccelli wines, to prove herself as a capable, responsible adult, and now this man was going to send it all tumbling down. Despite her father's support and confidence, she had seen firsthand too many times the havoc a public scandal could wreak. "I've seen those shows. I know what's going to happen."

"I'm not going to do that. Trust me."

"Trust you? That's what I did before. And look where it got me." She shook her head. Every reporter she had ever known would see a story like this as the break of a lifetime.

"And where is that?"

Damn, this man was frustrating. Why couldn't he just leave her alone? Just go do what he was going to do, and stop making her wait in suspense? "What are you talking about?"

"Did you even watch the show tonight?"

She shook her head. "I lived it. That was enough."

"Well, that explains a few things." A smile curved across his face, one she wanted to wipe away. Didn't he understand what this was going to do to her? To the store?

"Is this just one more story for you? One more notch in your reporter belt?"

"Not at all. In fact, I think this is the most important story I've ever covered."

His easygoing attitude infuriated her. He clearly didn't care. "Why did I ever trust you?" She tried again to turn away, but he refused to let her go.

"Matt dug in my files, and pulled out that research. Not me. I didn't give it to him. Carrie, I haven't done anything that would make you not trust me."

"Yes, you have. You—" She paused, searched for the times when he'd lied. He hadn't lied, exactly, but he had let her down. She had trusted him, and he had broken that trust. "You promised me it would all be okay." Her voice broke on the last words. She realized now how much that had hurt. "And it wasn't. At all."

"I know. And I'm sorry, Carrie. And I'm doing everything I can to make up for that. To change… everything." Night birds called to each other from somewhere behind them, while the party continued, laughter rising and falling in waves. Daniel let out a long breath, then released her and dropped onto the swing. "A long time ago, I broke the most critical promise of all and ever since, it seems like that's all I ever do—break promises."

She eased onto the empty space beside him, drawn by the vulnerability in his voice. Maybe she was judging him too harshly. And maybe, if she heard him out, she'd understand. "Why?"

He looked away, and she could feel the pain and regret coming off him in waves. This wasn't just about what had happened between them, it was about so much more, something over a year in the past.

"I should have been there," he said quietly. The words seemed to scrape past his throat. "I should have been home on time, like I promised her."

"People get tied up at work all the time, Daniel. You can't beat yourself up for that."

He shook his head. "I should have called a damned sitter. Hell, I should have turned down the assignment." A long, harsh gust of air exploded from his lungs. "Most of all, I should have thought about my family instead of my damned career."

"You are now, though, and that's a good thing. Annabelle—"

He whirled toward her. "Don't you understand? I *wasn't there* when she needed me. It didn't matter if we were separated. When Sarah called, I should have shown up to take care of my child. And every day since, I've said the words 'I promise,' and never kept them. I've just kept letting down my daughter again and again. And now…" His gaze met hers. "I let you down, too. Not on purpose, but it happened all the same. I thought I had it under control, but I didn't. I'm sorry, Carrie. You have no idea how sorry I am."

She tried not to cave to the pain she saw in his face, the regret in his features. But the part of her that still cared about him wanted to reach out, to comfort, to soothe. Wanted to believe him. To…love him. "Oh, Daniel, you're only one man, doing the best you can."

"You were right. I was putting my career ahead of the people I cared about. I was only focused on one thing—restoring my reputation. Living up to the Reynolds legacy." He said the last with a touch of sarcasm. "It was all I ever thought I wanted. Until I met you."

He kept talking, the words a waterfall pushing over the cliff of his mouth. "I tried, but it wasn't enough. Not that night. Not since then." His voice broke now, the sounds shattering like ice crystals falling off the side of a building. "I…failed them, Carrie. Dear God, I let them down. I am so, so sorry."

"You didn't let anyone down. You were human, that's all." But he didn't hear her words, didn't absolve himself.

"If I had been there, if I had put my family first—" He shook his head. "I should have…oh God, I should have."

And then he was in her arms, and she was holding him tight, and telling him he hadn't failed at all, that he was a good man, and that she understood. And he was apologizing over and over, until his voice went hoarse. His tears dampened her shoulder, and she went on holding him, letting him release the pain that had held him hostage for a year. If she did nothing else for him before she returned to Uccelli, she could do this.

After a while, Daniel drew back. She could see a clarity in his eyes, as if finally confessing his guilt brought absolution. "I'm sorry."

"For what? For letting a friend comfort you?"

"Is that what we are, Carrie?" His gaze searched her face. "Friends?"

The word hung between them. *Friends.* Was that what they were? she asked herself. Answering yes would be a lie. Saying no would open up a whole other door that she wasn't sure she wanted to open again. So she took the coward's way out and changed the topic. "You've been through a lot and though I can't begin to say I know what you're going through, I want to be there for you, Daniel."

If he noticed she didn't answer the question, he didn't say anything. "From here on out, I don't want to make promises I can't keep. Never again. I've let Belle down a hundred times since that day, and I don't want to do it again."

"She said you had a tea party with her."

He smiled, and she could see the regrets ebb a little more. "I did. I even wore the boa."

Carrie laughed. "You? Really?"

"Yup. I figured it was high time I showed my daughter how I felt about her. Proved to her that I was listening to her needs. Ever since my wife died, I felt like I couldn't be a good dad. I was gone so much when Belle was little that I barely knew her. My own daughter and it was like I was a stranger. I didn't know the names of her stuffed animals. Her favorite cereal. Her favorite book. But ever since you came along, I've learned to pay more attention."

"Me?" Carrie pushed off with her feet. The swing moved slowly back and forth, its soft *creak-creak* joining with the sounds of laughter and the birds, creating its own natural song. "What did I have to do with anything?"

"You slipped into her world as easily as diving into a pool. You hardly knew her, but still you found common ground. And she was happier and better for it."

"We're girls." Carrie shrugged. "It's easy to find common ground."

"And she and I are related, so it should be easy for us, too. But it wasn't. It was harder than hell and I felt like such a failure. I've just been—" he shook his head, let out a curse "—afraid."

"You?" She looked at the tall, confident, strong man beside her. One who had braved fires and gunshots to get the story when he'd worked in New York. She couldn't imagine ever using that word to describe Daniel Reynolds. "Afraid of what?"

"Afraid of letting down the people I love again. I kept thinking that if I didn't get too close, if I kept my focus on my job, it'd be easier." His stormy eyes locked on hers. "Easier than risking my heart…and falling in love."

The words hit her like a wall of ice. She jerked away from Daniel, sending the swing arcing back. "In love? Don't say that, Daniel, not if you don't mean it."

He got to his feet and came to stand before her. With one hand, he stopped the swing. With the other, he hauled her up and brought her within inches of his chest. "I do mean it, Carrie."

How she wanted to believe him. But she'd trusted him once before, and let this man into her home, into her heart. Where had it gotten her? On a television show that could ruin everything. How could she be so sure he wouldn't betray her again?

Her gaze rested on the dancing flames in the fire pit far across the yard. Orange and yellow warred for dominance, each hungrily licking at the logs steepled in the center. The fire could have been her heart—and the war inside her between want and common sense.

Damn, how she wanted him. Wanted to believe him. But still he held ammunition in his pocket, and she couldn't quite let her heart go again. He was wrapping her in his spell, trying to get close, she told herself, because he wanted the story. Not her. She returned her gaze to his and asked the question they'd both been dancing around. "Tell me the truth, Daniel," she said. "How long are you going to wait to betray me and ruin my life?"

CHAPTER FOURTEEN

DANIEL stared at Carrie, confused. Didn't she understand what he had done? "Wait for what?"

"Before you air the piece about my real father. A day? A week? A month?" She bit her lip, and tears glimmered in her eyes. "Just get it over with, Daniel."

"I'm not airing it. Ever."

"What are you talking about?"

"I'm not going to air it," he repeated. "In fact, that footage no longer exists." She truly hadn't seen tonight's episode. Otherwise she wouldn't be saying this.

"I was there, Daniel. I saw the cameras running. I just wish I hadn't been so stupid and I'd kept my mouth shut when Matt confronted me."

"You're not hearing me, Carrie. The footage doesn't exist anymore. Your story is safe." He reached for her hands and held tight. "Trust me. It's gone."

Still, she resisted. He could see the disbelief lingering in her chocolate eyes. "How did you do that?" she asked.

"I went in this morning, did some creative editing of the piece and slipped that into the queue to run tonight instead of Matt's disaster. And while I was there, I just happened to delete the other footage. And shred my notes. Something I should have done in the beginning when I realized I was falling for you." A grin spread across his face. Thank God Ted had been on board with the plan—not just on board, but enthusiastic about it. Seemed the young production assistant had had his run-ins with Matt—and Matt's lack of morals—as well. Ted had been more than happy to get back at Matt, and in the process, get credit for editing a quality news piece.

"But…but that could get you fired."

"I already quit." Daniel shrugged. He'd thought it would bother him to lose his job, but it didn't. Working for a boss he disliked in a job that grated on his conscience wasn't a career. It was a prison sentence. He would land on his feet no matter where he went from here, he was sure. "I might get sued, but I think not."

"They're just going to find a way to recreate it or come out with the story anyway."

"Nope. I took care of that, too."

"How? Come on, Daniel. This is the media. They're an unstoppable train."

"Unstoppable unless you know something bigger about them than they do about you." He couldn't believe he hadn't thought of this idea earlier. But at least he had thought of it in time. That was all that mattered. Carrie's story was safe, and he'd do it all over again if he had to, just to protect her.

"What are you talking about?" she asked.

"Turns out Mr. Miller, your grumpy customer and my mother's neighbor, knew something about my boss, Matt. He's Mr. Miller's nephew-in-law, and apparently he's not the Harvard grad he made himself out to be. In fact, he didn't graduate from any college. He was kicked out for plagiarizing a term paper. The station's owner, who prides himself on being a Harvard guy, wouldn't take kindly to finding out about that. And Matt knows it. He only got the job because of the Ivy League connection. After talking to one of the other employees, I found out Matt's done a few other shady things while working for *Inside Scoop*." The list Ted had given him had been long. Paying off sources, creating scandals when there weren't any, setting up interview subjects by putting them in a room with someone paid to create a stir.

"You blackmailed him?"

"I'd like to call it convincing him that it was in his best interests to let this go." Daniel had no doubt Matt wouldn't last long at *Inside Scoop*. The shady producer had seen the writing on the wall, and was probably emailing off his résumé right this minute.

Daniel had enough ammunition against Matt to create a sensational story of his own. One he could sell to the national networks. And in the process, save his career—or get the same one back. But that powerful urge to unearth the truth at any cost had died in Daniel and he knew that meant it was time to move on to another field.

"I could use that information to get a big exposé, get back on the networks," he said, "but I don't want to. If there's one thing you've taught me, it's the importance of being true to yourself."

"I taught you that? How?"

"By being true to who you are."

"True to being a fraud?" She turned away. "I don't think so."

"Do you think blood is the only thing that makes you part of a family? Even a royal family?"

"Maybe not, but—"

"There is no but. You are a princess. In my eyes, in

this town's eyes, in your country's eyes. And especially in Annabelle's eyes."

The last broke her heart. Somehow, she had to make it up to the little girl.

"If you act like a princess, you will be in the world's eyes, too," Daniel added.

"Act like one?" Carrie sighed. "You know me. When have I ever acted like a princess?"

"When you got on that plane and went to Winter Haven and took on a project that you loved. One that would bring the best of your country to the world. When you stood up for what was important to you and to your country. You are an ambassador, whether you know it or not. And isn't that what you told Annabelle a princess did best?"

Carrie shook her head. An ambassador didn't create a scandal on television. An ambassador held her tongue and kept her counsel. "I don't know about that."

"My daughter has said it to me so many times, I can repeat your words by heart, or at least do a good job paraphrasing." He grinned. "'Being a princess isn't about being the daughter of the king or being kissed by a prince. It's about being a good person, one who takes care of the people she loves and stands up for what's important to her.'" His smile softened. "You said that, Carrie, and it's true."

"Maybe, but—"

"No buts about it. You stood up for what you believed in when you took the chance on coming to this country and running the wine shop. When you got on that show and showed the world that a real princess doesn't have to embroider or speak French or do whatever it is supposed real princesses do. That she can be a working woman with a fabulous business under her.

And when I saw you do that, I knew that I had to stand up for what was important to me, too."

Her eyes were wide and glistening under the moon-light. "And what is that?"

"Family. The people I love. I want what I said a minute ago. Keeping my promises to the people I love is more important than anything else. Than any story, any job." He had realized that last night, when he'd been sitting at the small table with Annabelle. He wanted nothing more than to make his daughter smile and laugh like that, every day for the rest of his life. And he couldn't do that until he had righted the wrongs he'd done to Carrie. "I made a promise to you, Carrie, when I started this. I told you it would be okay, and now, it will be."

She bit her lip. "What are you going to do now?"

"Well…" His smile widened and his thumbs traced the back of her hands. "I thought I might get married."

"Get…" She shook her head, as if she hadn't heard him right. "What?"

"Married. Though I have to admit, I may not be that good a catch, considering I'm currently unemployed."

"I'm sure you'll find a job. You're very talented." She broke away from him and turned toward the swing. "You'll make some woman very happy."

He came up behind her, so close he could feel the heat emanating off her body, watch the whisper of his breath catch on the tendrils of her hair. "Is it really that hard to trust me?"

She turned back to face him. "I trust you."

He arched a brow. "Carrie, darling, you don't trust anyone."

"Of course I do."

The brow arched a little higher, calling her on her lie.

She sighed. "Okay, you're right. I don't trust people easily. And reporters…"

"Are the hardest to trust of all."

"Yes."

He winced at the truth. He could see why she thought that, even about him. He had earned that title of untrustworthy as surely as some of his colleagues had. In the quest for the story, there were casualties in relationships both casual and long-term.

No more, Daniel decided. He wasn't that man, not for one more second.

"I understand that because I've been on both sides of the equation. Matt used me, like he would any interview subject, to get the scoop he wanted. I thought I could keep the lid on it, but I should have known better. He's a ruthless man who wanted fame and fortune at any cost. When I saw him do that, I knew I could no longer be that kind of person. I realized how badly you were going to be hurt—not just you, your family, your country, your family's business—by one foolish moment twenty or more years ago that never should have seen the light of day, so I took action."

"What's to stop someone else, someone who was there and overheard everything, from going to the papers?"

"Nothing." He wished he could erase memories as easily as he had the digital recording. "But we'll deal with that if and when it happens. *Together.* Any scandal that comes our way, we'll beat it back."

He could still see the doubt in her eyes. "Daniel, I don't think—"

He pressed a finger to her lips, cutting off her objections before she could voice them. "You don't trust anyone, because no one has ever seen or known the real you. But I have, Carrie. And the real you is pretty damned fantastic."

"It's only been a couple of weeks since we met. How can you possibly know me in that short a time?"

"I know that you are a determined, strong woman who will take whatever risks she needs in order to protect what she loves. You are a princess, through and through. Not the kind of princess who goes around wearing a crown and pitching diva fits, but the kind of princess you described to Annabelle. You take care of the ones you love, and you stand up for what's important to you. Not to mention, you're honest and sweet and loving, and most of all, you have Annabelle's vote." He grinned. "If you ask me, that's the most important vote of all."

"Vote for what?"

"To be my wife."

Her mouth opened. Closed. Opened again. Had she heard him right? "Your...wife?"

"There's only one woman I want to marry." He waited a beat. "And that's you, Carlita Santaro."

Daniel's words sank slowly into Carrie. They settled into her veins, then her heart. Her gaze met his and in those blue eyes, she saw truth. A smile curved across her face and filled every ounce of her. "This amazing, courageous and incredible man wants to marry me...a regular girl?"

He laughed. "You, my dear, are far from regular."

"And so are you. From the minute I met you, well, maybe the second time I met you—" she grinned "—I knew you were different. I saw you reading that story to your daughter and I saw a man with heart and soul. A man who will do whatever it takes to protect the ones he loves. And you have done that with me."

"Because I love you, Carrie." He reached up and traced a hand along her jaw. "The tiara's just a bonus."

She laughed, joy bursting in her features like new flowers in spring. She had taken a risk, one far bigger than the one she'd taken in coming to America, and it had worked out. The man she had met and fallen for truly was the prince she'd dreamed of finding. "Oh, Daniel, I love you, too."

Laughing, he drew her to him and kissed her. Thoroughly, deeply, their mouths joining in a dance that could barely contain the love between them. Her hands went around his back and she held tight, loving him right back. A long moment later, Carrie pulled back. She could feel the happiness radiating from her face and the tease dancing on her lips. "And what if I never wear the tiara again?"

"I don't care. As long as you wear my ring." Daniel took a deep breath, then reached into his pocket and pulled out a small black velvet box. He hinged back the lid to display a princess cut diamond, flanked on either side by a half dozen smaller champagne diamonds. He'd had to try three jewelry stores before finding the exact ring he wanted, but when he saw the surprise on her face, he knew it had been worth every moment of the hunt.

"It's…stunning, Daniel."

"I wanted something that had a little of you and a little of Uccelli in it," he said. "The champagne diamonds are nearly the same color as the pinot grigio that brought us together in the first place."

She put a hand to her mouth. Tears welled in her eyes. He really did understand her and appreciate all sides of her. How had she gotten so lucky to meet a man that loved both the commoner and the princess sides of her? "It's so perfect."

He dropped to one knee before her. "Is that a yes? You'll marry me?"

"I…" A wide smile curved across her face and she started nodding at the same time she whispered, "Yes. Yes, Daniel, I'll marry you."

Joy burst inside him. He wanted to shout the news from where he stood, scream it to the world. Instead, he rose, kissed her again and slipped the ring onto her left hand. The stones caught the light of the moon and seemed to wink their approval.

He raised Carrie's hand in his and pressed a light kiss to her fingers. "You know, I've read a lot of fairy tales with Annabelle. In the end, the prince always gets his princess and they ride off into the sunset on his noble steed. But—" he feigned disappointment "—there's one problem with our fairy tale."

"What's that?"

"I'm not a prince."

"I'll let you in on a secret," she said, pressing her lips to his, "I'm not really a princess, either. But I don't think that's going to stop us."

"From what?"

She curved into his arms and laid her head on his chest, seeming to become a part of him. "From living happily ever after."

"And they did," he whispered, lowering his lips to hers, "forever and ever."

* * * * *

Harlequin Romance

Coming Next Month

Available October 11, 2011

You can find more information on upcoming
Harlequin® titles, free excerpts and more at
www.HarlequinInsideRomance.com.

HRCNM0911

REQUEST YOUR FREE BOOKS!
2 FREE NOVELS PLUS 2 FREE GIFTS!

Harlequin

Romance

From the Heart, For the Heart

YES! Please send me 2 FREE Harlequin® Romance novels and my 2 FREE gifts (gifts are worth about $10). After receiving them, if I don't wish to receive any more books, I can return the shipping statement marked "cancel". If I don't cancel, I will receive 6 brand-new novels every month and be billed just $4.09 per book in the U.S. or $4.49 per book in Canada. That's a savings of at least 14% off the cover price! It's quite a bargain! Shipping and handling is just 50¢ per book in the U.S. and 75¢ per book in Canada.* I understand that accepting the 2 free books and gifts places me under no obligation to buy anything. I can always return a shipment and cancel at any time. Even if I never buy another book, the two free books and gifts are mine to keep forever.

116/316 HDN FESE

Name	(PLEASE PRINT)

Address	Apt. #

City	State/Prov.	Zip/Postal Code

Signature (if under 18, a parent or guardian must sign)

Mail to the **Reader Service:**
IN U.S.A.: P.O. Box 1867, Buffalo, NY 14240-1867
IN CANADA: P.O. Box 609, Fort Erie, Ontario L2A 5X3

Not valid for current subscribers to Harlequin Romance books.

**Are you a subscriber to Harlequin Romance books
and want to receive the larger-print edition?
Call 1-800-873-8635 or visit www.ReaderService.com.**

* Terms and prices subject to change without notice. Prices do not include applicable taxes. Sales tax applicable in N.Y. Canadian residents will be charged applicable taxes. Offer not valid in Quebec. This offer is limited to one order per household. All orders subject to credit approval. Credit or debit balances in a customer's account(s) may be offset by any other outstanding balance owed by or to the customer. Please allow 4 to 6 weeks for delivery. Offer available while quantities last.

Your Privacy—The Reader Service is committed to protecting your privacy. Our Privacy Policy is available online at www.ReaderService.com or upon request from the Reader Service.

We make a portion of our mailing list available to reputable third parties that offer products we believe may interest you. If you prefer that we not exchange your name with third parties, or if you wish to clarify or modify your communication preferences, please visit us at www.ReaderService.com/consumerschoice or write to us at Reader Service Preference Service, P.O. Box 9062, Buffalo, NY 14269. Include your complete name and address.

HRI1B

Harlequin Romantic Suspense presents the latest book in the scorching new KELLEY LEGACY *miniseries from best-loved veteran series author Carla Cassidy*

Scandal is the name of the game as the Kelley family fights to preserve their legacy, their hearts...and their lives:

Read on for an excerpt from the fourth title
RANCHER UNDER COVER

Available October 2011
from Harlequin Romantic Suspense

"**W**ould you like a drink?" Caitlin asked as she walked to the minibar in the corner of the room. She felt as if she needed to chug a beer or two for courage.

"No, thanks. I'm not much of a drinking man," he replied.

She raised an eyebrow and looked at him curiously as she poured herself a glass of wine. "A ranch hand who doesn't enjoy a drink? I think maybe that's a first."

He smiled easily. "There was a six-month period in my life when I drank too much. I pulled myself out of the bottom of a bottle a little over seven years ago and I've never looked back."

"That's admirable, to know you have a problem and then fix it."

Those broad shoulders of his moved up and down in an easy shrug. "I don't know how admirable it was, all I knew at the time was that I had a choice to make between living and dying and I decided living was definitely more appealing."

She wanted to ask him what had happened preceding that six-month period that had plunged him into the bottom of the bottle, but she didn't want to know too much about him. Personal information might produce a false sense of intimacy that she didn't need, didn't want in her life.

"Please, sit down," she said, and gestured him to the table. She had never felt so on edge, so awkward in her life.

"After you," he replied.

She was aware of his gaze intensely focused on her as she rounded the table and sat in the chair, and she wanted to tell him to stop looking at her as if she were a delectable dessert he intended to savor later.

Watch Caitlin and Rhett's sensual saga unfold amidst the shocking, ripped-from-the-headlines drama of the Kelley Legacy miniseries in

RANCHER UNDER COVER

Available October 2011 only from Harlequin Romantic Suspense, wherever books are sold.

USA TODAY bestselling author

Carol Marinelli

brings you her new romance

HEART OF THE DESERT

One searing kiss is all it takes for Georgie to know
Sheikh Prince Ibrahim is trouble....

But, trapped in the swirling sands, Georgie finally
surrenders to the brooding rebel prince—yet the
law of his land decrees that she can never
really be his....

Available October 2011.

Available only from Harlequin Presents®.

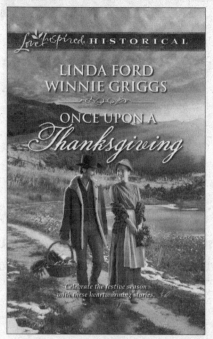

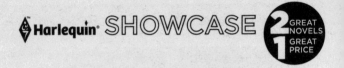